Texans' Tall Tales
by a Tall Texan

By JE Warr

This is a work of fiction, Historical individuals and places and events are mentioned. Villages are actual names, places. All other characters, locales, and accounts of events are fictional and are entirely the product of the imagination of the authors, and any similarities are purely coincidental.

For Information, address
rseibert@advancedconceptdesign.com
axlerod@peoplepc.com

First e- print September 2025 ASIN:
Paperback print September 2025
ISBN 13: 978-1-965535-17-2
Printed in the United States of America

Contents

You Know You've Met Someone Special If Years Later You Can't Remember If They Were Real or A Dream

Chapter 1: Stuka

I was five in 1953, our small East Texas town of Longview felt like the edge of the world, where pine forests whispered secrets and every sunrise promised adventure. My dad, a large ex-Marine with a mischievous grin and an addiction to things that scared him, was an adrenaline junky. He craved the spark that lit our wild escapades. Each weekend, he'd wake me before dawn, his eyes glinting like the first star in the sky, whispering, "We have a DTM Mission, 'Don't Tell Mom'.

I'd scramble after him, heart racing, ready to chase the unknown.

Our adventures weren't zoo trips or Sunday drives. We hunted snakes with sticks in misty forests, the air thick with pine and earth, my stick a knight's sword missing every slithering target. We climbed steep hills to a secret waterfall, its spray cool on our faces as Dad whooped like a kid. Once, we teetered across a rickety swing bridge, the creak of ropes matching my pounding pulse, as my daddy made us swing to the protest of the ropes. Each outing was a thrill, a secret forged between us, sealed with "Don't Tell Mom" to keep Mom happy. She never understood adventures, Dad said, and we'd do anything for her smile but that five foot 2 red head had a temper to avoid more than any snake.

One time, after watching *Superman*, I asked Dad if he could fly. He said he could, but Mom had taken his cape and hidden it. I just happened to have a red towel I figured would work fine. I tied it around my neck, climbed onto the roof, and jumped. Let me make two things clear: 1) I didn't tell Dad about my red towel plan or jumping off the roof, and 2) red towels don't slow your fall one bit. Dad probably saved my life—he had old lumber piled against the wall, and when I landed on it, it broke my fall instead of my neck. If not for the nail that punctured my leg, Mom would never have known. That's when she started talking about sending me to a "special school." She had me tested and they said I was fine.

One morning, Dad's grin was wider than usual. "Double DTM, kid," he whispered. "We're flying my new plane." My stomach flipped. He'd told Mom we were fixing a friend's boat in Marshall—a friend I'd never met, a boat I'd never seen. We drove east of Longview on Highway 80, the road cutting through towering pines to a hidden airstrip. There it was: a red Bellanca with black-striped wings, its sleek body gleaming under the Texas sun, the faint whiff of aviation fuel mixing with fresh-cut grass. A tractor hummed nearby, trimming the field, and that grassy scent lodged in my memory, forever tied to that plane.

We pushed the plane to the runway's edge, Dad looping a rope that looked speciously like Mom's clothesline he tied it to the tail around the tail wheel and rapped it around a fence post, threading it to the pilot's seat. "Like driving a car, just in the sky," he said, winking, as if flying was no big deal. I stood under the wing, heart thumping, as he yanked the propeller. The engine roared, shaking my bones. Dad sprinted to the door, yelling, "Hop in!" I scrambled inside, the engine's growl filling my chest. When he released the rope, we shot forward, as the propeller disappeared in a whirl. The runway blurred, my stomach lurching as we neared the edge. We lifted off, but Dad cursed softly; the wind was wrong.

We looped back, reset the rope, and tried again, this time going into the wind and soaring into the sky. The world below turned tiny, a patchwork of green and gold, more beautiful than any tree I'd climbed. The wind whistled past, carrying the scent of grass and rope, and I felt like we'd conquered time itself. We'd fly to the clouds, and I'd stick my hand out to touch them, as if they were huge, fluffy white mountains. We'd circle around them. Dad worked for the Texas and Pacific Railroad and used his railroad experience to navigate, always flying over the tracks. One day, we flew far from Longview. I asked if we were lost. "I might not know where I am, but I'm never lost!" he said. He told me to look for a water tower, since back then, they always had the town's name painted on them. I spotted one in the distance, and we flew low, circling to read the name, Dangerfield.

Every weekend, we "fixed the boat," but really, we flew. Dad let me fill one of Mom's pillowcases with rocks, and over Lake Cherokee, we played "Stuka," diving at logs like German dive bombers, my rocks splashing wildly. Dad laughed, calling me his ace bombardier as he hollered, "Bombs Away!" I named the plane *Stuka*, proud of our secret missions. One day, mid-dive, the engine sputtered and died. The propeller came back into sight and froze, a silent blade against the clouds. My heart pounded, but Dad's voice was steady: "No problem." We were low, the dam below a narrow strip barely wide enough for the plane. A windsock fluttered, its red and white stripes snapping, guiding us down. I gripped the seat, my pulse a drumbeat, as Dad eased us onto the dam with a gentle thud—no hops, his smoothest landing yet. "Told ya," he said, winking, as I let out a shaky laugh, adrenaline buzzing.

A farmer plowing nearby sold us five gallons of gas for $10—highway robbery, but Dad just shrugged. The farmer asked if we flew a seaplane, chuckling. "No," I piped up, "that's a *Stuka*!" Dad grinned, adding, "A damn *Stuka*." They roared with laughter, but I didn't get the joke. The farmer held the tail as Dad revved the engine, and we took off like a turtle in a thunderstorm. In the air, Dad leaned over, voice low: "This is a Double Secret DTM." I nodded, solemn, knowing Mom could never know. Later on my dad found out that that lever on top of the cockpit was to turn on the reserve gas tank.

Our *Stuka* days ended at my grandmother Mammy's house. Mammy was strict—no tree-climbing, no rock-throwing, no matches. My sister Wynn and I were in her backyard, on a tree branch tossing rocks at lit matches to douse them, when Dad's plane buzzed overhead. "Daddy!" we shouted, waving. Mammy stormed out, caught us, and somehow, Wynn swears it wasn't her but she spilled the truth about the plane. Mammy's "significant" conversation with Dad was fierce, but he charmed his way through, claiming a friend gave him the plane for "boat work." He planned to sell it for a profit, he said, and buy my mom a new Lincon.

Mom's reaction was quieter but sharper. Her eyes narrowed, lips pursed—the "mom look" that could stop a tornado. The air grew heavy, her floral perfume mixing with the scent of fresh coffee and Marlboro cigarettes. "How'd you fly without a license?" she asked. Dad pulled a worn book from his pocket: *How to Fly an Airplane*. "Read this," he said, grinning. "Flew to Shreveport, landed, and told them I needed a license. The instructor, also a Guadalcanal veteran, tested me and said, 'Us Jarheads are a different breed." Mom shook her head, demanding the title and keys. "Sell it," she said. "We're getting a new car." The *Stuka* became a gray 1950 Lincoln, which Dad called a Sherman Tank. I think he missed the Stuka.

Years later, Mom and I laughed about that day. "Why'd you let him lie?" I asked. She smiled, soft but wise. "Jimmy, I love your dad. Sometimes we "dance"—he knew I saw through him, but I let him save face. It's what you do when you love someone's wild heart." I didn't understand then, but I do now. Dad taught me to chase the unknown, to feel the rush of a propeller's roar or a dam's narrow landing. My dad taught me to love adrenaline as it is the only glue to a smile and to ring every ounce of life out of every moment and never quit. Mom taught me the dance— she taught me that the best way to get a kitten to love and come to me was to let it go when it wanted to leave. She showed me how to love without taming, to balance adventure with trust. Every time I smell fresh-cut grass, I'm back in that red-and-black plane, soaring with Dad, our secrets safe under the Texas sky. And every kitten reminds of "The Dance".

Let's keep this string going, usually, our family reunions were quiet affairs except for the lynch mob my aunts formed to string up my dad.

Chapter 2: The Lynch Mob

An enchanting force seemed to draw all the male relatives to the front of the lake house, entranced by a mystical pull they couldn't resist. The air crackled with unseen energy, as if whispers of ancient incantations filled the atmosphere. Their senses tingled, as if a soft, ethereal breeze brushed their skin. The spell cast a hazy veil over their minds, leaving them no choice but to succumb to its command. It tapped directly into their masculinity, heightening their senses and leaving a lasting impact. No matter what the task was at hand, the moment it appeared, everything stopped. Conversations cut off abruptly, objects were set aside, frozen in time. They were drawn to it like sirens song.

The annual 4th of July Warr family reunion took place at Lake Cherokee, just outside Longview, Texas, at my grandfather's sprawling lake house. The house had a wraparound screened porch, stood two stories high, and boasted a dance room with its own piano and a swimming pool, despite being on the lake. Though only a few carried the Warr surname, me to be exact, my grandfather came from a family of 12 siblings, but he was the only son—those sisters were a force to be reckoned with in Center, Texas. No dance could begin until the "Warr Party" arrived. They were the forerunners of a girl gang, incredibly productive, finding partners and fueling the Baby Boom with a yearly reunion of at least 100 people.

My Uncle John's arrival on a 1947 E-model Harley-Davidson Knucklehead was the magical event that captivated the men and pulled them to the front of the lake house. The air seemed charged with otherworldly energy, signaling something extraordinary was coming. At the end of the driveway, John leaned into a turn off a tar road his motorcycle roaring beneath him.

The sun's rays danced on every inch of chrome, casting a dazzling spectacle. The seat, studded with chrome, glistened in the radiant light. Even over the party's lively music, the Knucklehead's electrifying potato, potato potato thump—still capable of sending shivers up anyone's leg—resonated through the air. As Uncle John halted and swung his leg over the seat, a captivating mix of scents filled the air: supple leather intertwined with the earthy fragrance of Harley oil, drifting effortlessly through the crowd.

The men gathered around the stunning Harley, captivated by its gleaming fishtail pipes and the luxurious feel of its chrome-studded seat. The motorcycle's impeccable design, paired with the looping thump of its engine, heightened the anticipation and excitement. They had a "man crush" on Uncle John, eyes fixated as he strutted in black leather lineman boots, his World War II fighter cap perched atop his head, radiating nostalgia.

In that moment, a seed of fascination was planted in my young, impressionable mind, destined to flourish for a lifetime. The men's vibrant expressions, the murmur of their voices, and the mix of anticipation and excitement left an indelible imprint. The women sensed danger; the men sensed adventure.

Sixty-five years later, my dad's face is etched in my memory, his eyes filled with awe and desire, as if he could taste the excitement. It was like a siren's song in *Ulysses*, a promise of things to come, evoking desire, temptation, and the allure of intellectual and carnal risks.

The motorcycle gleamed under the sunlight, its chrome reflecting the admiring faces around it. The engine's roar was a symphony of power and freedom. Even with the engine off, the shimmering heat was magnetic. I can still feel the electricity in the air, the palpable longing for something more, drawing us to the open road.

My dad was a great car salesman, and that day, I saw him work his magic. As he picked me up and set me on the fringe-and-chrome-studded seat, he told John what a great motorcycle rider he was. I'd never seen him ride a motorcycle, but he claimed he was a motorcycle messenger in the Marines. John, convinced, gave him permission to take it for a spin.

Dad tried to remove me from that seat so he could ride alone, but there was no budging me—not even with a John Deere tractor. He whispered sternly that I couldn't come, his voice laced with authority. Determined, I shot back, reminding him I'd tell Mom our secret if he refused. I'm sure he pictured her reaction. Once Mom got wind of his plan to ride a motorcycle—well, all you married men know what he was thinking. So, he sat down, moved me in front of him, and at the ripe age of five, I learned I was a pretty good salesman myself.

The 1947 Harley-Davidson Knucklehead had a tank shifter and an aptly named suicide clutch operated by the left foot. After a few pointers from Uncle John on starting and stopping the beast, and a few kicks, the Knucklehead roared to life. Man, the sound and vibration were both horrifying and thrilling. After stalling twice, Dad reassured my now-worried uncle that he was "a little rusty." With me in front, we took off with a screech of the rear tire and a screen of smoke.

Ten seconds into that twisting tar road, I fully appreciated its sheer coolness. The vivid colors, electrifying noise, subtle aroma of the tar, and exhilarating rush merged, etching an indelible memory. I struggled to catch my breath against the relentless wind. At the first turn, Dad didn't slow down, he gave it more gas and leaned over. I've spent my life chasing that

rush of leaning a motorcycle, the wind howling as we sped around a corner. After a right-hand turn came a left-hand turn, straightening up and leaning again, why would anyone drive a car?

Before we got upright, we hit a stop sign with gravel on the road. I'm not sure why, but we crashed. It was our first time on a motorcycle, for both me and my dad, he had never ridden one in his life. The crash unfolded in agonizing slow motion. The screech of gravel on metal pierced the air, drowning out all else. The pungent odor of burning rubber and smoke overwhelmed my senses, adding to the chaos. I could almost feel the impact reverberate through my body, as if time slowed to capture every detail. Dad, doing what he called "his job," let go of the handlebars, wrapped his arms around me, and pulled me tight, holding me even as we hit the ground and skidded to a halt. With the Harley on its side, the back wheel spun, the engine roaring at full throttle until the last drops of gas vanished from the tilted carburetor. Before standing, he rubbed his bloody hands over my head, arms, and legs, asking, "Are you OK? Are you OK?" I'd never seen him so worried, his brows furrowed, hands trembling as he checked me. His pants were ripped at his bloody knees, his shirt torn, elbows scraped raw, hands covered in blood.

I didn't have a scratch. I tried to lift the Harley but couldn't budge it, so I sat on the roadside. Dad grabbed the bike, kick-started it, the engine's roar filling the air as he revved the beast. Concern etched his face; worried fear would overtake me. He extended his bloodied hand, and amidst the metallic scent, asked again, "Are you alright?" I said, "Yes, let's ride some more," jumped back on, and enjoyed the ride home as much as the ride out.

You might think this was a terrible accident, but it was nothing compared to the disaster when we returned to the lake house. Before Dad could make me swear our DTM (Don't Tell Mom) oath or wipe his blood off me, I ran to tell Mama and my aunts about my big motorcycle ride and wreck adventure.

The first aunt I reached was Aunt Gisler. Bursting with joy about the adventure, I exclaimed, "My daddy took me on a neat motorcycle ride, and we crashed!" It never occurred to me that the blood all over my body and head, where Dad had touched me, might terrify her. It's hard to understand an excited five-year-old, but she caught "MOTORCYCLE CRASH" loud and clear. She rallied all the women, and once they confirmed I was unhurt, they turned like a military precision unit, marching toward Dad with clenched fists and curses on their lips. Aunt Dovey led the charge. At maybe four-foot-five, she was a furious force. You can't fathom how fast 30 or 40 beer-drinking aunts and mothers can form a mob mentality. Aunt Lovey was tying a hangman's knot in a rope she found. I don't know where they got those pitchforks.

I saw something in Dad's eyes I'd never seen before. A Marine at Guadalcanal and Okinawa, he once said it was like "being run through hell and beaten in the face with a dead rabbit." Those Japanese couldn't have been as terrifying as the mob closing in. Dovey, too small to get in my six-foot-two father's face, nipped at his ankles like Mom's Chihuahua.

Then came an awful sound, like a grizzly's roar, as the mob parted for the maddest, redheaded mama bear anyone's ever seen—my mom. Her temper could intimidate Al Capone. She was so mad at Dad she was crying, and her tears made her madder still. Anger doesn't even touch her rage. Amid her inaudible curses, she spotted Dad's bloody condition and screamed, "Where's Jimmy, you bastard?" After hugging me tightly and seeing the blood, I thought we'd need an ambulance for her until I convinced her it was Dad's blood.

Soon, every woman and girl kissed and hugged me. Once satisfied I was okay, they joined the chorus asking Dad, "What were you thinking?"

All 11 aunts were in the music room, dancing, drinking, and playing the piano before the ruckus. One aunt would play, and when she tired, another would slide in mid-song, seamlessly taking over. They used this "one out, one in" system on Dad, like a giant swarmed by enraged yellowjacket wasps. I was a coward—I wanted to wrap my arms around him to protect him like he had done me but I feared getting stung. Dad couldn't take it anymore, so he ran and jumped into the lake.

When he emerged much later, the aunts had lost interest and stopped throwing rocks when it was clear he was out of range. They wandered off, and he joined the men on the screened-in porch, all hoping the women's animosity would fade. Dad started bragging about how tough his boy was, saying he'd call neighbors to warn them before letting me out to play. He looked at me with pride, raised his fist like he was going to fight, and said, "Isn't that right, Jimmy?" Then he took a fake swing. In that moment, I did what every woman there wanted to do I balled up my little fist and struck him square in the groin with such force he doubled over, groaning in pain. Everyone ran over at the sound. Uncle John, still mad about Dad wrecking his motorcycle, recounted the events, saying Dad deserved it.

That got everyone laughing as Dad lay in agony. The aunts softened, trying to comfort him, though their laughter made it hard to speak. It probably didn't make Dad feel better, despite their empathy.

As a result of that reunion, Uncle John never brought his motorcycle to another family event, and my "tough" reputation was so established that no one, not even the big kids, messed with me. There were countless times things went awry, but I'll always cherish the security I felt when Dad embraced me, shielding me from harm. He passed on something I've tried to do with my own kids, because "That's my job."

Dad's next wild scheme? Something loud, fast, and laced with pyrotechnics that lit up the Pinetree Elementary School—and assaulted the principal."

Chapter 3: Hot Rod Lincoln Memoir

When I was a kid, my dad, Jake Warr, wasn't just a man—he was a force of nature. A Marine from Guadalcanal with a gleam in his eye and a hunger for things that went fast and loud, he lived life like he was born to burn rubber. His pride and joy was a Model A convertible. I say convertible, but it had no top, no fenders, no muffler, no hood; it did, however, have whitewall tires because I helped my dad paint them on. It turned heads wherever we roared. It had a Lincoln flathead V8 motor growling like a panther with a belly full of dynamite. Dad always said, "Any fool can restore a vintage car, but it takes a real man to chop one up." And chop it he did, inspired by the rockabilly anthem *Hot Rod Lincoln*, a song that thumped through our house like a heartbeat, its lyrics about speed and swagger fueling his soul.

I'd climb into the passenger seat, grinning like a fool, as Dad taught me to handle the stick shift with the precision of a gunslinger. "Smooth, kid," he'd say, his voice low and steady. "Feel the car, don't fight it." Together, we'd tear through town, the engine's deep rumble shaking the pavement, chasing the horizon like it was ours to catch. That car wasn't just a ride; it was a rolling testament to Dad's love for noise, speed, and showing off.

One day, Dad decided to crank the spectacle up a notch. He rigged spark plugs to each exhaust pipe, with an old phone coil positioned under the seat. When he revved that flathead engine to its screaming limit, the car vibrated like it was possessed, filling the air with the smell of gasoline and the promise of chaos. "Ready for the show, kid?" he'd ask, his grin wild as he killed the motor, letting raw gas pool in the pipes. You'd think it was over, your ears ringing, your nose tingling with exhaust. But then—flick—he'd hit the coil switch, and BOOM! Flames shot out the back, four feet of pure dragon's breath, followed by a thunderclap that shook the night. I'd whoop and holler, "Again, Dad!" while he laughed like a kid who'd just set off his first firecracker.

Some folks might call that stunt crazy. Me? I was six, and it was the coolest thing I'd ever seen. The night we finished the flame-throwing rig, we named it "Spitfire" and couldn't wait to test it. At 12:45 AM, with the neighborhood fast asleep, we were out in the driveway, Dad revving the engine and me shouting for more. Each explosion lit up the night, the booms echoing off houses like cannon fire. Mom, a fiery five-foot-two redhead who'd been married to Dad's antics for a decade, was used to his shenanigans. But the neighbors? Not so much. By 1:00 AM, their phone calls poured in, shrill and furious. Mom stormed out, her face glowing redder than her hair, and let loose a tirade that could've peeled paint. "You two morons, go to bed—NOW!" she bellowed. I felt proud that she included me in the Moron Club. Dad, still in his work boots, didn't argue. When Mom's temper flared, it was like staring down a volcano. We slunk inside, but I couldn't stop giggling. Later, as we sat in the quiet garage, Dad nudged me. "Worth it, right?" he whispered. I nodded, still buzzing from the thrill.

A week later, I was at Pine Tree School, bragging to anyone who'd listen about Dad's flame-throwing *Hot Rod Lincoln*. Word spread like wildfire, and by the end of the day, a hundred kids were buzzing about Spitfire. When Dad pulled up after school, a cheer rose from the crowd. I didn't have to beg much—Dad was a born showman, and I was his acorn, not falling far from the tree. "Show 'em the flame trick!" I pleaded. He smirked, revved the engine until it screamed, the vibrations rattling our bones and forcing kids to clap their hands over their ears. "Here we go!" he shouted, pumping the accelerator to pool fuel in the pipes, then hitting the coil. BOOM! Six feet of fire roared out, the heat smacking every kid in the face. The crowd went wild—until the flames licked a patch of dry grass along a fence, setting it ablaze.

Panic ensued. Twenty kids stomped out the fire with their little feet, but not before the fence was a smoldering ruin. Dad and I bolted like our hair was on fire, thinking we'd made a clean getaway. But kids talk, and my so-called friends ratted us out faster than you can say "detention."

The next day, the principal summoned us to his office. We sat in the outer room, me perched in a chair big enough to swallow me whole, Dad standing like a Marine awaiting orders. The principal, a bow-tie-wearing bureaucrat behind a mahogany desk the size of an aircraft carrier, started yelling about responsibility and property damage. Big mistake. Dad, who didn't take crap from anyone and wasn't known for his latitude, reached across the desk, grabbed the man's bow tie, and yanked him over. Papers, a lamp, and a nameplate crashed to the floor with a bang—not as loud as Spitfire's exhaust, but close. Dad stood him up, nostrils flaring like the flames he'd unleashed the day before. "You want to talk to me like a man, we'll talk," he growled. "You want to yell, we'll fight. Your choice." The principal, feet dangling, made the smart call. He apologized, Dad set him down, and then, cool as a cucumber, stuck out his hand. "Hi, I'm Jake Warr. Now, what'd you want to see me about?" We walked out scot-free, but Mom wasn't so forgiving. She grounded me for a week and made Dad repair the school's fence, grumbling the whole time.

That *Hot Rod Lincoln* wasn't just a car; it was Dad's masterpiece, a roaring tribute to the song that set his heart racing. Every time he cruised down the street, flames or no flames, he'd grin, knowing he'd brought a rockabilly legend to life. And me? I was just proud to be the kid in the passenger seat, shifting gears like he taught me when he said, "Shift." I was always chasing the next adventure with the man who taught me life's too short to take crap—or drive slow. I am Jake's acorn.

Our next adventure was somewhere over the rainbow.

Chapter 4: On My Way to Oz

My dad was just seventeen when he lied about his age and enlisted in the Marines, shipping off to the South Pacific—Guadalcanal—where war showed him its ugliest face. He survived a sniper's bullet that grazed his ankle, leaving a jagged scar he'd later call his "lucky mark." He watched comrades fall in the jungle; their names etched in his memory. Those close calls with death taught him life's fragility and left him with a fierce gratitude for every breath. He'd say, "Kid, you gotta' grab every moment like it's your last." That war shaped him, fueling a zest for life that could light up even the grayest day.

Whether it was spontaneous road trips or savoring a sunset, Dad approached everything with contagious excitement. His laughter filled the room, and his curiosity led him to tinker with anything, knobs, gadgets, you name it. That fearless spirit sparked some wild adventures, like the time he decided to conquer the skies with a weather balloon, I know that didn't make sense to me either.

One day, while flipping through *Popular Mechanics*, he spotted an ad for a full-size weather balloon, boasting high-altitude capabilities and durable material. "This'll be bigger than the Fourth of July!" he said, eyes gleaming, as he filled out the order form. Every day after, he checked the mail like a kid waiting for a birthday gift. When the package arrived, he grabbed me before opening it, knowing I loved tearing into boxes. "Go on, rip it open!" he urged, bouncing like it was Christmas morning. Mom, less thrilled, put her hands on her hips and shook her head. "A weather balloon? You don't even watch the weather on TV!"

In the backyard, Dad rigged an adapter to our gas meter—duct tape, garden hose, and pure ingenuity. "This is for science," he winked, tapping the hose before it hit the meter. (The statute of limitations on gas theft's long expired, so we're safe.) He fed the hose into the balloon, pinching it to control the flow. At first, it looked like a deflated puddle, but as it filled, it grew huge, swaying like a giant jellyfish. When it started straining skyward, Dad worried it might pop. "That's enough," he said, pulling the hose out and tying a rope to the balloon. Gas spewed everywhere, so he handed me the rope. "Don't let go, no matter what," he warned, sprinting to shut off the valve.

Ten feet away, the balloon yanked me upward. I soared five feet off the ground, screaming, picturing Dorothy in *The Wizard of Oz*—but I wasn't letting go of Dad's dream. He spun around and leaped, grabbing my legs. We crashed to the ground, laughing as the balloon kept climbing. For half an hour, we watched it shrink to a dot through his binoculars. A week later, he claimed folks in France found it. "Don't feel bad, kid," he whispered. "And DTM; it was our code for, Don't Tell Mom!" His tall tales always grew wings, but they kept our secrets safe.

Mom wasn't fooled. She grounded me for a week, (I never learned exactly what being grounded meant) and she made Dad mow the neighbor's lawn as penance, muttering about "that damn balloon." He just winked at me, mouthing, "DTM." He always caught me whenever I flew too high, pulling me back from danger's way with a laugh. He'd seen life's fragility in Guadalcanal's jungles, but he taught me to chase its joys—full throttle, no regrets, and always with a smile.

We soon moved to the dusty wilds of El Paso, Charlie Deming sparked epic chaos—from darting neighbors and sand-skiing on junk hoods to shooting me (mostly forgiven). These tales paint a hilarious portrait of boyhood mischief gone legendary. Dive in and feel the gunpowder thrill!

Chapter 5: Charlie Deming the Shootist

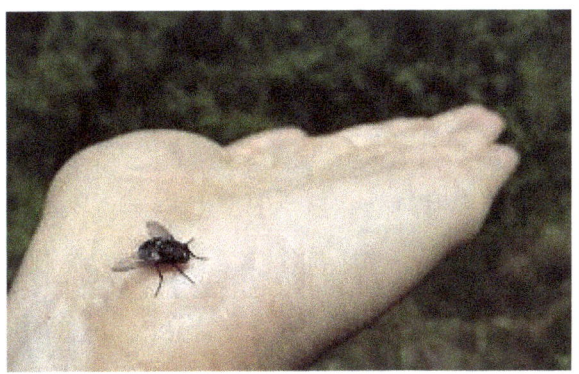

Sometimes, a collection of tales, woven together like a vibrant tapestry or a word mural, is needed to paint a vivid portrait of an individual. Charlie Deming is one of those special people. Picture this: the overpowering odor of gunpowder lingering in the air.

Let me start by saying he's one of only two people who've ever shot me—but let's not rush ahead. I mention this upfront just in case you sense any lingering animosity. I'm certain I've moved past it by now. Mostly.

Charlie and his brother George lived next door to me on Cork Street in El Paso. Living so close to me was quite an experience. I'll admit I could be loud and obnoxious at times, but Charlie, oh boy, had his own unique way of being obnoxious—just not loud. Take, for instance, our neighbor Danny, pedaling his bike through the narrow space between Charlie's house and mine. Out of nowhere, Charlie hurled a dart, hitting Danny square in the left buttock. The agonizing impact drew a piercing scream, like a distressed pig who "cried wee, wee, wee, all the way home" in the fairy tale. When Danny's enraged mama bear appeared, her massive form casting a shadow, Charlie's heart raced. The air thickened with tension as he faced the consequences. In a panic, his words spilled out, voice ringing with fear: "I didn't know the dart was loaded!" The unmistakable scent of fear wafted through the air. If he thought that would calm her, he was mistaken, she'd lost her sense of humor. Charging forward, she raised both hands, crimson-painted claws ready to strike. Lucky for Charlie, mama bears, with their powerful paws and massive frames, can't scale rock walls. Charlie, a master of "wall huddling," pressed his back against the rough surface, heart pounding, feeling the coolness of the rocks. His ragged breath echoed, mixing with the distant rumble of angry pursuers. I knew I'd be safe—having my own mama bear—so I ran to find her and swear I had nothing to do with the assault, even though I knew the dart was loaded. Danny's mom formed a posse of neighborhood mothers, but Charlie lay low for a week until it blew over. I only saw him outside once, disguised as an ugly girl with a wig and all. As you can see, I'm not the least bit prejudiced just because he shot me.

To be fair and balanced, I must confess: Charlie also shot himself. We lived on the far east side of El Paso, where the desert started across the street and stretched for hundreds of miles—a young boy's playground. My dad and I built a dune buggy from a '53 Studebaker—more on that beast later. Charlie and I roamed that desert, shooting guns and dreaming up trouble. One day, we stumbled on a rusted 1950 car hood and saw its potential. We invented *sand skiing*, a sport so wild we figured it'd be Olympic bound. We chained the hood to the dune buggy's back, and Charlie perched on it like a king while I floored it. The engine roared, sand stung his face, and the gritty rush made us howl with laughter. That thrill—turning junk into glory—was my first taste of spinning something ordinary into a legend, a trick I'd later master on the open road. The hood heated up fast, so we slapped cardboard down to dodge the "butt burn." But the desert's relentless sand chewed through the metal, leaving Charlie sliding on raw grit. He came up unscathed, grinning, but we dubbed him "Smooth Butt Charlie" for a spell—though he ditched that name quick.

No matter how hard you search today, the desert from El Paso to Carlsbad, New Mexico, holds no trace of a single car hood. We burned through them all, their rusted souls lost to the fleeting glory of sand skiing.

Let me preface the next story with a revelation. I used to believe people never change, only our perceptions of them shift. I was wrong. People evolve, like the metamorphosis I've undergone. Today, I won't step on a spider, I'll trap a yellow jacket in a glass and release it outside, and on walks, I avoid ants. But back then, Charlie and I roamed the desert hunting small game. The scorching sun beat down as we treaded through arid sand, my single-action .22 revolver strapped to my leg. The wind whistled through the desolate landscape, mixing with distant coyote yelps. The scent of dry earth and greasewood filled the air, reminding us of our harsh surroundings. I'm not proud of it now, but we targeted lizards, their swift movements blending with shimmering heatwaves, challenging our marksmanship. Charlie, aiming to impress, went for an even smaller target, a persistent fly landing repeatedly on his hand. Each swat sent it flying, only for it to return. The buzzing of its wings mingled with the dry heat, the arid air intensifying the moment. I suggested he make it land on his head, picturing myself as William Tell, ready to shoot it off. Charlie hesitated, doubting my aim or his trust in me. My William Tell dream faded. He liked the idea but insisted on doing it himself. Sure enough, the fly returned to his left hand. With deliberate slowness, he raised his rifle, right hand trembling slightly. The metallic click of the safety echoed in the still air. His squinted gunfighter eyes locked on the tiny target. I hadn't noticed the kitchen match in his mouth—there should've been harmonica music to amplify the tension. He aimed at the fly. Too late, I realized I was in the line of fire. The acrid scent of gunpowder tickled my nostrils as my heart pounded, I just knew that if he hit that fly with a Long Rifle 22 it's body would stop the bullet but if he missed I'd be shot. I leaped aside just in time.

The bullet obliterated the fly, leaving a lingering whiff of gunpowder. Charlie stared at the black, smoking spot on his hand, a searing heat from the gunpowder burned embedded under his skin. I couldn't suppress my laughter; unaware

Charlie didn't find his folly amusing. Little did I know he was plotting revenge.

Eastwood High School, years in the making, was finally complete. Alongside it, they'd built a top-notch football field with bleachers and lights for night games. The lush green grass and crisp yard lines were matched by a high-quality synthetic track with eight lanes, marked for various events. It was a source of pride for the community, hosting local and regional meets. Charlie and I decided to check it out, so I drove us in my dune buggy.

Adrenaline coursed through my veins as I stepped onto the track, the scent of fresh rubber in the air. The new surface was a siren's song, inviting me to test its limits. The special gravel, designed for traction, was a NASCAR enthusiast's dream. Walking to my Studebaker dune buggy, I imagined roaring engines, cheering crowds, and breakneck speeds. Today, I'd channel my inner "Fireball" Roberts and chase my dream of becoming a legendary racer. I told Charlie to get out and time me. I wanted to go down in history as the first to set the fastest lap (a record I still hold).

With the engine roaring, I approached the first turn, gripping the steering wheel. I yanked the to the left, sending the buggy into a controlled slide. The rear swung out, time slowing as I maneuvered inches from the turn's edge. The electrifying sensation surged through me, etching the memory deep. My lap times, recorded by Charlie's Timex, got faster each round.

Charlie's eyes lit up with excitement as he saw the grooved track. I motioned him closer, eager to share the thrill. He stepped onto the track, feet sinking into the grooves, a grin spreading as he felt the freedom. We laughed, the shared joy bonding us. But as Charlie took the wheel, Coach Gotcher, a tall, athletic man, ran onto the field, cursing like a sailor and gesturing for him to stop. Charlie's heart pounded, adrenaline surging. The dry, hot desert air burned his lungs as he sprinted across the nearby desert, Coach Gotcher close behind, footsteps echoing. The uneven terrain challenged him, but Charlie's determination fueled his escape. Glancing back, he saw the coach faltering, gasping in the heat. The gap widened until Gotcher was a distant figure in the shimmering haze. I seized the chance to jump in the dune buggy and head into the desert, passing a winded Coach Gotcher, hands on knees, too breathless to look up. I picked Charlie up, and we sped home. He acted mad, furrowing his brows and crossing his arms, but I explained I didn't make him drive. "If you hadn't stopped me," I pleaded, "Gotcher would've been after me." I saw realization dawn as he processed my words. He'd saved me from trouble, and our tension eased—or so I thought until he shot me.

This story's no longer short; it's a semi-short saga. I'm reminded of my preacher friend Bobby Orozco, who'd say, "And in conclusion," meaning not a damn thing. I promise to wrap it up.

Flipping through the musty pages of the *World Book Encyclopedia*, their scent filling the air, I hunted for a gunpowder formula. The crackle of turning pages sparked my curiosity. Understanding a boy's love for explosions is key. I studied an early Chinese gun, a simple bamboo tube. Clutching a quart of homemade gunpowder, sulfur teasing my nostrils, I sought Charlie, the only one who shared my blazing passion. Between our houses, we stuffed a firecracker into a metal tube, added an inch of powder, and I found carpet tacks in the garage—sharp, bullet-like, perfect. Charlie cut a coat hanger into a ramrod, pushing a tack into the barrel, topping it with torn newspaper. I aimed the "bazooka" skyward as Charlie lit the fuse. A loud boom echoed, the tack whizzing through the air. We tried again, Charlie holding the tube, me lighting the fuse. It hissed, but nothing happened; the smoke faded. The firecracker was a dud. As Charlie lowered the barrel, I turned to find something to dislodge it. A deafening explosion shattered the air, a searing pain engulfing my right hand. Blood pooled, but I stayed tear-free. Charlie claimed his mom called him, but I heard only ringing in my ears. He sprinted off, a coward leaving me bewildered.

I was always mischievous, often in precarious predicaments. That day, I couldn't recall the wild tale I'd planned for Mom—some adventure with friends—but it slipped my mind. Since I always aim for truth, I won't fabricate now. Mom, no stranger to Dad's antics, knew better than to press me. She'd helped raise him, with his elaborate escapades, so she valued mystery. Smiling knowingly, she let me off without interrogation—a silent agreement that some stories stay untold. I felt profound gratitude for her wisdom. She wrapped my hand in a dish towel and rushed me to St. Thomas Hospital's emergency room. They cleaned me up and sent me home. Four years later, thinking I'd fractured a finger while playing football, Mom took me to the doctor. After an X-ray, he asked if I'd held a carpet tack. The ER hadn't checked four years prior—the tack was still in my hand. I needed surgery to remove it. Thanks, Charlie.

Looking back, I don't hold a grudge—much. Charlie was a spark in a dry desert, setting every moment ablaze. I like to think he's out there, dodging coaches and angry moms, maybe with a smoother butt and better aim and a black spot on his hand. These stories are my tribute to a kid who made El Paso feel like the Wild West, tack and all.

Charlie was a spark in a dry desert, setting every moment ablaze with his reckless ideas. That same fire lit something in me—a hunger to spin tales as wild as our stunts, to turn a dusty road or a speeding ticket into a story that could stop you in your tracks. Years later, out on the lonesome highways of West Texas, I'd weave a yarn about a hitchhiker and a phantom chief that'd make Charlie proud. But that's another tale, one where stupid is king.

Next three friends play Russian Roulet.

Chapter 6: The Crash of a Non-Running Go-Cart

I can't reflect on the foolishness of my youth without recounting the legendary tales of Dr. Bob Bryant, PhD (in stupid things), the unrivaled king of stupidity. The inventor of that old Texas saying, "Watch this!" Bob had an addiction shared by many Texans: he was an adrenaline junkie. Whenever he tried to appear ordinary, his addiction relentlessly dragged him back to his natural state: "Abby Normal." He needed at least one dangerous experience a day, or he'd go into withdrawal. I've seen him, on a day without danger, clench his fist and punch a roll-top desk, breaking his hand. The memories come alive with vivid images of his reckless escapades, echoing laughter, the lingering scent of adventure, and the exhilarating rush of each foolhardy act. He embodied the traits of a large, aggressive, barrel-chested adrenaline addict, believing that if something didn't scare him, it wasn't worth doing.

During my junior year at Eastwood High in El Paso, I stumbled upon Bob, our paths crossing as neighbors living just a stone's throw apart, though the precise details of our initial encounter escape me. He appeared in my life as if by magic, blending in like a wicked stepbrother who materialized out of thin air and was accepted as family. Don't get me wrong, I'd do anything for him. Bob embodied hyperbole in every step, each feature exaggerated to the extreme. His wide, vibrant eyes pulsated with electric intensity, always eager for the next adventure. His voice, soft and brief, forced you to pay attention to his muttered words, because those words could spell your doom.

The peculiar thing was his use of Jade East cologne—its musky, spicy scent wafted through the air, lingering long after he'd gone, like putting a bow on a pig. His demeanor exuded firmness and forcefulness yet left an indelible impression of aggression. In every way, he was an extravagant character plucked from reality. Bob was fully committed all the time. If you looked up "wild hair," you'd find a picture of Bob in his immaculately pressed bleeding madras short-sleeve shirt and chukka boots. Corralling my mind to write this is challenging, as every sentence sparks another memory of his impulsive ideas. I'm known for stretching the truth now and then, but this stuff really happened. I'm confident Ken Chamberlain, Bob's neighbor, will back me up, as he took part in most of it.

Ken was Bob's next-door neighbor. Younger than Bob and me, Ken became a close friend, largely because of his captivating sister, Ricki. When Bob saw the attractive new neighbor moving in, he reacted with excitement, jumping like a kangaroo on a trampoline. He made his way to Ricki, introducing himself and wasting no time asking her out. He even carried her refrigerator into the kitchen on his back to make a good impression. She went out with him twice, but Bob's charm faded fast when he took her to the Border Town Drive-In. They sat in the cluttered, worn-out interior of Bob's filthy '55 Chevy, its faded paint covered in grime. The musty scent of stale French fries and engine oil mingled with the faint smell of wet dog. As the engine roared to life, the clanking metal and rumbling exhaust echoed through the rusty frame—a testament to the hole he'd chopped in the muffler with a hatchet. He'd owned that turd for a year, but it looked like decades of neglect had passed. For some reason, its dilapidated state made him proud. He bragged about never washing it.

On their second date, while waiting in line at the Border Town Drive-In, some suicidal fool cut in front of one of the most dangerous men in El Paso. Bob had peculiar behavioral quirks: if he found something on the ground, he'd pick it up and hold it to his ear. If he caught you with your head near the ground, he'd "kick-start" your head by pushing it into the dirt with his foot, a move he learned from watching professional wrestling. If someone cut in line, he'd give them what he called a "head honking." Ricki pleaded with him to calm down, but Bob was unyielding, like a horse with the bit in its teeth—there was no stopping him until blood was spilled. He pulled the fool out of his car through the driver's window and explained the folly of his actions with his persuasive fist, grabbing the guy's neck and smashing his nose with his right hand. He never worried about the police; his father, Hilton, head of the Liquor Control Board, expected deference from law enforcement due to his lofty position. You might say Bob showed Ricki his true nature, and her interest found no purchase in it. That was their final date, but somehow Bob and I became responsible for her little brother, Kenny Chamberlain.

Bob and I were about 18, and Ken was just 13 when we connected, but the three of us did everything together. I don't know how much we influenced Ken's young mind, but he turned out fine—except for his habit of holding things to his ear when he finds them on the ground.

One day, Bob called and said, "Come over—we're gonna have some fun." When Bob said "fun," it usually meant someone was getting hurt. When I arrived, Bob and Ken were standing beside the turd in the middle of the street, with Bob's non-functional go-kart parked near the rear passenger door. His go-kart, once a competitive machine, had met its demise in a race in Juarez and

was beyond repair. Still, Bob wanted to test its speed by making a sharp turn onto his street from the long, straight Album Street. He tied a lawnmower starter rope to the right door handle of his filthy '55 Chevy. "I want you to tow me to the end of Album," he said. "I'll hold the rope, then

we'll turn around, and you can hit about 40 mph."
He explained he'd tow Ken at 45 mph next, then
me at 50. Bob always went first, so I drove, and
Ken acted as safety engineer, ensuring I didn't
accidentally run over Bob—because that would
only make him mad. Nobody wants to be around a
mad Bob Bryant. Given his quirks, Ken and I
jokingly planned that if I ran over him, I'd back
up and do it again—twice should be enough to
finish him off.

I got Bob up to 40 mph, and he let go of the
rope, skidding through the turn—cool! Next was
Ken at 45 mph, and again, it was fun. Then it was
my turn at 50 mph, and thanks to my exceptional
driving skills, I made it look easy. That challenged
Bob, who was eager to push the limits of a non-
running go-kart with racing suspension. I'm still
baffled why we didn't see that exceeding the
"limit" of a right-hand turn would cause a crash.
We were like three fools playing "Russian Go-
Kart Roulette" for kicks.

Bob claimed he could handle 65 mph. I
doubted it, but I knew cautioning him would only
spur him to try 70 mph, so off we went as fast as
the turd could go. Ken warned me the moment
Bob released the rope and crouched behind the
wheel that there was no way he'd make the turn—
and he was right. Bob refused to accept he was
going too fast and never touched the brake. He

started on the right side of the street, hugging the curb to lessen the angle, but slid sideways into the left curb at nearly 60 mph. It's nearly impossible to describe the chaos that followed. Bob and the go-kart kicked up an immense cloud of dust, swirling with sticks and chunks of weathered concrete. The scene was a cacophony of crashing noises, mingled with the smell of dust, blood, scraped flesh, and gritty debris in the air. On every rotation, a tire or elbow popped out of the painful, engulfing cloud until everything slammed into an outhouse backed by a rock wall. The collision broke his momentum but not before the outhouse exploded, releasing the blue, smelly remains of its toilet bowl.

We rushed over to check if Bob was alive, and he was barely breathing. After a minute, he started making a sound like a cat coughing up a hairball. We planned to drag him back to his house but didn't want to touch him. We grabbed a long cushion from the lawn furniture and used 2x4s to lever him onto it without making contact. Then we dragged the cushion, with him mostly on it, along the sidewalk to his garage. We carried him through the garage and placed him on the kitchen floor, as he'd requested, fearing his mother would kill him if he bled on the carpet—or if the smell of the outhouse remains lingered. His mother, a five-foot, 95-pound woman, probably couldn't have done much damage. We then returned for the go-kart, which was too bent to roll—only three tires touched the ground at once. If you stepped on the airborne tire, another corner would lift. So, we carried the non-running, non-rolling go-kart into the garage.

Just then, Bob's dad, Hilton Bryant, drove up. The best way to describe Mr. Bryant is stoic and dry. He approached the mangled go-kart, placed his wing-tipped shoe on the elevated right front tire, and pushed it down, causing the left rear wheel to jump up about a foot. Without a word, he shook his head, walked into the kitchen, straddled poor, bleeding Bob, and said, "I'll be damned. You wrecked a go-kart that doesn't even run. You remind me of stock." He then pushed Bob's bloody foot aside, grabbed a beer from the fridge, and went to the den to watch a baseball game.

We figured it was best to let Bob explain his version of events, so we took off. We didn't hear from him for about a week. During that time, we considered moving to Alaska. Ken saw Bob four days later, picking at his scabs and planning his next adventure. He told Ken, "That was cool."

I don't know how to put a ribbon on this pig, so just trust me and read on.

Chapter 7: Change the People Around You—or Change the People Around You

A grizzled old biker, after watching Bob and me get the shit stomped out of us, leaned over a bar counter, his beard smelling faintly of motor oil and regret, and rasped, "Son, there comes a time when you gotta change the people around you—or change the people around you." I didn't get it then, but my best friend Bob, with his knack for dragging me into chaos, made it crystal clear.

Our friendship was a runaway freight train, and I'd just found the emergency brake.

Bob's been a moron since the day I met him, and I'll confess, I wasn't exactly Einstein myself. We were two peas in a pod, tearing up the backroads of El Paso with "street racing", living by the racer's creed: "You ride as fast as the people you ride with." Another racer, a grizzled veteran with scars like a roadmap, once warned me, "If Ride with your pants down, kid, and you're gonna get fucked." By my twenty-first birthday, I was trying to pull my pants up, metaphorically speaking, and fix my "stupid." But Bob? He had a PhD in "re-stupiding" me. Every time I swore off dumb decisions, Bob's grin reeled me back into the idiot vortex.

Take the time he called, voice buzzing with that manic energy that screamed trouble. "Let's hit the Super Modified races in Albuquerque!" he said. "Three-hour drive, triple digits, your Corvette convertible. I got a great idea." Bob's "great ideas" usually ended with someone dialing 911 or hiding

from the law. But did I listen to the warning bells? Nope. I was still the guy who thought, *What's the worst that could happen?*

I pulled up to Bob's place in my Vette, top down, engine purring like a contented panther. She was long, lean, and high-geared for speed—

hotter than a $2 pistol. Bob sauntered out, sporting an evil smirk and a duffel bag that looked suspiciously heavy. He vaulted over the door—because Bob never used a door when he could make an entrance—and landed in the passenger seat with a thud. "What's in the bag, man?" I asked, eyeing it like it might bite.

"You'll see," he said, grin widening. "Just drive."

This wasn't my first rodeo with Bob's mystery plans. Last time he had a "great idea," he roped in me and his neighbor Ken, a scrawny kid whose ears made him look like an International pickup truck coming at you with its doors open. Bob had borrowed his mom's Opel station wagon. Why? "Because it's got a luggage rack," he said, like that explained everything. Next thing I knew we were at the city dump, wrestling a Caterpillar tire the size of a small moon onto the roof. It took all three of us, grunting and cursing, to hoist that beast up—we could've used three more guys. The Opel sagged like it was begging for mercy, tires squealing in despair, and the transmission's fourth gear flat-out refused to cooperate as we chugged up Scenic Drive, a winding road that snakes up Mt. Franklin in the middle of El Paso.

At the top, Bob, eyes gleaming like a kid about to set off fireworks, announced his plan: "We're gonna roll this tire down the mountain." It was like something out of *Lonesome Dove*, where Gus chases buffalo just for the hell of it. Watching a giant tire careen down a mountainside? That's the kind of dumb that sounds fun when you're young and invincible. We didn't even glance at the houses dotting the base of the mountain. What could go wrong, right?

The tire took off, bouncing and roaring like a prehistoric beast. It smashed through a stone wall, which slowed it enough to only dent the house it hit instead of leveling it. As the dust settled, reality kicked in. "Bob, we gotta get the hell, outta here!" I hissed. "Cops will be swarming!" We piled into the Opel, driving oh-so-casually down the mountain, banking on the fact that no one would suspect a creaky station wagon of hauling a monster tire. We got away clean, but that poor Opel's been leaning left ever since, like it's still traumatized.

I told you evert thought of Bob reminds me of another story so let's get back to where I left off with Bob and me and a bag of rocks and bottles on our way to Albuquerque. You'd think I'd have learned. My dad used to say, "What do you learn the second time a mule kicks you?" Then he'd answer himself: "Not a damn thing!" And there I was, proving him right, cruising toward Albuquerque with Bob and his mystery bag.

After thirty miles, Bob unzipped the duffel, revealing a stash of rocks, bricks, and glass bottles. "What the hell, Bob?" I demanded.

He grinned like a cartoon villain. "The bottles? I wanna see if I can chuck 'em at road signs and stick the neck through without breaking the glass. The rocks and bricks are for when I run out. Gotta work on my aim at seventy miles an hour."

I should've pulled over right then. I should've kicked him out. But part of me—the part still infected with Bob's brand of stupid—thought, *Hell, that might be fun.* "Why my car?" I asked.

"Convertible's better for overpass signs," he said, like it was obvious. The hair on my neck should've stood up, but it was probably too tired from all the other times Bob dragged me into madness.

We hit I-25 near Las Cruces, and Bob zeroed in on an overpass sign—clearance 16.8 feet. "Damn that 16.8!" he growled, like it had personally offended him. He grabbed a bottle, stood up in the passenger seat, and hurled it with the force of a major-league pitcher. The thing sailed way too high, disappearing over the overpass. I glanced in the rearview as we shot out the other side—and saw the bottle arcing back toward us like a boomerang from hell."Bob, you idiot!" I slammed on the brakes. The bottle smashed on the pavement just ahead, spraying glass like confetti. Bob turned to me, eyes wide with fake innocence. "Oops," he said. "That was cool!"

Cool and stupid—the two words that defined Bob. I decided right then to plot my revenge.

Opportunity knocked a few miles later. Bob was rummaging through his bag, picking his next projectile, when I spotted a pickup with a walk-in camper ahead. Perfect. I gunned the Vette to ninety, closing the gap fast. Bob didn't even look up. Just as we got close—way too close—I yanked the shifter's T-handle and made a machine-gun noise, *brrrat-tat-tat*, like we were in a dogfight. Bob's head snapped up, and at that exact moment, the camper's back door flew off— some freak pressure change, I guess—and flipped over us, missing the car by inches.

Bob yelped, nearly dropping his precious bag of rocks. His face went white, and I swore I saw his soul leave his body for a second. I peeled away from the camper, grinning. "Oops," I said, mimicking him. "That was cool!"

We were still laughing, trading jabs like the old friends we were, when we rolled into Albuquerque for the races. It was a blast— screaming engines, burning rubber, the kind of chaos we lived for. But we were broke as usual, so, no motel for us. After the races wrapped at ten, we pointed the Vette back toward El Paso.

I was beat, so I let Bob drive. I-25 stretched out like a black ribbon, and my Corvette ate it up at a smooth hundred miles an hour. I was dozing, lulled by the engine's hum, when we dipped into No Gale Canyon, about fifteen miles north of Truth or Consequences, New Mexico. Something shifted in the air—Bob's vibe went from cocky to twitchy. I sat up, blinking, and glanced behind us. Holy shit! Red lights everywhere in the distance, like a swarm of pissed-off fire ants with sirens and little red lights on their heads. Bob had blown through a roadblock. "What the fuck, Bob?" I yelled. "What's going on?"

He shrugged, cool as a cucumber. "Nothin'. I'm just tired. Why don't you drive?"

"Fuck you, you asshole! You ran a roadblock! Floor it!"

Bob slammed the pedal, and the Vette roared like a dragon. We screamed into Truth or Consequences with a decent lead on the cops. Thinking fast, I spotted a convenience store with a walled-in dumpster area out back. "Pull in there!" I said. I jumped out, moved the garbage cans, and guided Bob as he backed the Vette into the tight space. We covered our tracks, replaced the cans, and strolled across the street to a 24-hour

McDonald's like we were just two dudes grabbing a late-night burger.

The cops tore through town, sirens blaring, lights flashing like a psychedelic nightmare. We munched on fries, trying to look casual while the manager glared at us. "This is a 24-hour restaurant, not a 24-hour motel, boys," he finally said. After an hour, when the chaos died down, we slipped back to the Vette and crashed in the seats. I made Bob sleep in the driver's seat—penance for his stunt.

At dawn, we took back roads to El Paso, dodging any more trouble. When we pulled up to Bob's house, I looked at him, his stupid grin still plastered on his face, and I knew I was done. "Bob, old buddy," I said, "this is the last straw. We're through."

I peeled out, leaving him standing in the dust. That was the last time I saw Bob. Part of me misses the chaos, the dance we did on the edge of disaster. But the smarter part—the part that finally pulled its pants up—knows I'm better off without him.

Goodbye to My Moron Friend, Bob

A wise man—probably my Uncle Huge, who dispensed life advice between sips of cheap whiskey—once told me, "There comes a time when you must change the people around you or change the people around you." I didn't know what he meant back then, but my longtime best friend Bob dragged me kicking and screaming to that crossroads. It was a one-way street with a big ol' "No Return" sign, and Bob was the guy waving me through with a goofy grin and a bad idea.

Bob's been a moron as long as I've known him, which is saying something because we met in 11th grade. We were two peas in a pod, "You ride as fast as the people you ride with." By my twenty-first birthday, I was trying to fix my "stupid." I wanted to trade my reckless ways for something resembling a future. But every time I tried to clean up my act, Bob was there, like a devil on my shoulder with a mullet and a Monster Energy drink, whispering, "C'mon, let's get re-stupid."

Next I prove … hell I don't even know why I did it but I confess, I did.

Chapter 8: The Falling Rocks Prank

Now you might call me devious or an asshole, but I want you to understand; My father was an equal opportunity prankster, he would pull a joke on his friends or a total strange, so it's part of me DNA.

He was a solitary figure standing on the side of the road with his thumb out, dwarfed by the enormity of the landscape like a BB in a boxcar. His name was Ray, and he wore a jersey that seemed as out of place in the desert as he did, a bright green and yellow shirt emblazoned with the name of some rugby club from Pennsylvania.

He carried an enormous pack on his back, but it seemed to me the heavier burden was his loneliness, or perhaps the realization of how far he was from home. I mean, rugby in Texas?

I picked him up. Maybe it was curiosity, maybe something else—an unspoken understanding that out here, on this lonely stretch of road, we're all just passing through, bound by the miles we'd driven and the ones still to come. In the desert, where silence stretches endless, stories are the only company you can count on. I'd told a few in my time, mostly to pass the hours, but something about Ray—his wide-eyed trust, maybe—made me want to spin a bigger one, to see how far a tale could carry us both. In Texas, you either hear a tall tale or your part of one; you're either the joke or the joker, but most Texans are just happy to have a tale to tell. You'll hear somewhere I'm the joke or the joker—I'm not trying to make you feel sorry for me; I'm trying to make you grin.

Ray spoke little at first, the road swallowing our conversation like the dust trailing behind the car. But eventually, he turned to me, eyes wide with the anxiety of being in an unfamiliar place. "Do I need a passport to get into New Mexico?" he asked.

I could've set him straight. But instead, I leaned into the story, tempted by the chance to shape his experience of this strange, vast world, if only for a little while. "No passport," I said, my voice steady as the wind against the windshield. "Just tell them you're a Mexican—they'll usually wave you through."

I watched his face, a mix of confusion and trust, a vulnerability that almost made me regret the tale. But the road has a way of loosening the tongue, and some stories, once begun, unfold on their own.

The moon hadn't risen yet when we passed through the vast oil fields. The wells burned off gas, lighting the night like ancient fires, reaching upward as if trying to touch the endless sky. I saw Ray's eyes widen with wonder at the flames, and I leaned into the story I hadn't yet finished.

"Chief Falling Rocks," I said, the name dripping with mock menace, like Jerry Seinfeld cussing out "Newman!" It seemed to rise from the darkness, a ghost of the landscape. "They say he and his band have been raiding these parts for years. Stealing cattle, burning ranches. They swapped their horses for dirt bikes, their bows and arrows for assault rifles. You see those flares out there? That's them, flickering in the distance, always moving, always just out of reach."

Ray's gaze stayed fixed on the flames. He clung to my words as if they were the only truth in this vast, indifferent world. And why shouldn't he? Out here, the line between real and imagined blurs with each passing mile.

As we neared Van Horn, that speck of civilization caught between desert and mountains, the land grew rockier, more uneven. There, on the side of the road, was a sign: "Watch for Falling Rocks." I could feel the tension in Ray's breath as he read it aloud, his voice barely above a whisper.

I didn't say anything at first. The weight of the story hung between us like the cool desert air. But as we passed the sign, I turned to him with deliberate calm. "They're out there," I said quietly, as if they might hear me. "Keep your eyes open."

Ten miles later, the full moon rose, glowing like an old incandescent porch light. I'd traveled this road fifty times and knew what was coming. A rest stop came into view, its huge teepees standing like silent sentinels over each picnic table. I flicked off the headlights and let the car roll in neutral. Silence enveloped us, except for the faint sound of Ray's breath catching, his hand gripping the door handle as if he might bolt into the darkness at the first sign of trouble.

For the rest of the drive to El Paso, Ray sat rigid, scanning the shadows, waiting for something to emerge from the mountains. His silence told me all I needed to know—the desert had come alive for him, teeming with unseen dangers.

We finally crossed into El Paso's glow, neon signs flickering into view, their light washing away the desert's shadows and the story I'd spun. "Well," I said with a quiet laugh, "that was close."

I wonder, even now, if Ray still remembers that night—if the land he traveled through took on a different shape because of my tale. I hope he found what he was looking for, whether it was the truth or something else entirely. And if you're reading this, Ray, I owe you a beer.

As you can see, I will not only prank a stranger, I prank a friend next.

Chapter 9: The VW That Got 1,000 Miles Per Gallon

You need to understand, I don't pull these pranks to hurt anyone—I do them to store up tall tales so when I'm old, I can tell them to you. Yeah, that's the ticket; I did it for you! That's my story, and I'm stick, stick, sticking to it.

My dad worked for Chevrolet Motor Division in El Paso, Texas, and when I graduated from Eastwood High School, he got promoted and moved with my mom to Dallas. I had already started college at UTEP (University of Texas at El Paso), home of the National Basketball Champions—you know, *Glory Road*. I needed a place to stay and found an apartment where my high school friend Kenny Smith (not his real name) was living. Kenny was a dope smuggler, dealing marijuana. Times were different then. The sixties were the beginning of a whole new world , you know Flower Power, free love, bell bottoms and Frisbees in the park, when a girl could hitch hike and not be killed Kenny lived on the second floor of a very old house owned by a very old Lebanese couple about a block from UTEP.

One day, Kenny Was an entrepreneur at a very young age and with Mexico right next door he started a business smuggling grass over the boarder He was looking for a place to stash his weed in the basement when he found an old furnace and figured it'd be a mighty fine spot for his 10 bricks. The old landlord, whom they called Uncle Tonoose after the Lebanese uncle on *The Danny Thomas Show*, saw the weed, thought it was trash, and burned it. Ten pounds of wacky tobaccy produces a lot of smoke. El Paso has an inversion layer, meaning the smoke rises about 20 feet, then lays down like a sick dog and waits for a dust storm to move it along. It didn't make the newspaper, nor did Pete Hainline, our favorite local newscaster, report it, but that was a special day at UTEP. It became known as "High Day." A *Guinness Book of World Records* entry was awarded for the most chocolate chip cookies eaten in one day, and nine months later, more babies were born on the west side of El Paso than ever recorded.

Kenny was coming home from class when he smelled it. He followed his nose, along with a couple hundred other baby boomers enjoying their noses too. They looked like a pack of blind dogs in a meat locker, spreading blankets and frisbees, with a small rock band camped around the house. Nobody saw the old couple—we think they were having sex. Kenny, fearing narcs waiting for him, split town like a jaguar with its tail on fire. If narcs were there, they were as high as everyone else, trying to score with the braless hippie chicks. Kenny told me he'd paid that month's rent, so I could move in—the old couple wouldn't even notice he was gone. The rent was only $100 a month.

It was a perfect spot, just a block from UTEP and cheap. It had two bedrooms, so I put a sign up at the Student Union Building looking for a roommate to split the rent.

I got a call from a guy with a funny accent named Tom Daughty, from Minnesota, he could have use close captions so I could understand what he said.. He seemed nice, so we shook hands, and he moved in. My girlfriend, Vickie, liked him too, and we all got along, except for one thing: I kept drinking his milk. Tom was a bit anal-retentive—my anil's scattered everywhere—but he needed his Capan Crunch and milk every morning. You know how those anal-retentive types act when there's no milk for their crunch. One night, he put a sign on the milk: "I SPIT IN THIS MILK!" So, I taped a note next to his: "So did I!" Now, I don't care who you are, that's funny.

Tom was a fraternity pledge, and his big brother, a guy named Costello, was a class-A asshole. One rainy day, Tom asked him, "Where's Abbott, and who's on first?" Costello made him stand in the parking lot yelling "ABBOTT!" for three hours.

Tom wanted revenge, so he asked Vickie to make her world-class Hatch green chili cheese enchiladas, with one special ingredient: Ex-Lax in Costello's portion. Vickie didn't want to do it—she's a nice person and didn't care about storing tall tales for when she's old—but Tom and I tag-teamed her, and she agreed. It got easier once Costello sat down and started bitching about El Paso and Mexicans. Vickie's half-Hispanic, half-German—a Chili-Kraut—and the more that asshole talked, the bigger she smiled, knowing what language his asshole would soon speak. The next day, Tom gave Vickie flowers, thanking her for the joy she brought him. I made him clarify what he meant. "Costello said he never shit that much in a week," Tom said. "He doesn't have a stomach for Mexican food." We laughed our asses off, and I just gave you the story I promised. I bet Costello never ate another enchilada.

Tom's parents bought him a brand-new VW Bug, which I thought was silly, gas was only 32 cents a gallon. I drove a manly 64 Corvette convertible. Uh-huh! He kept giving me shit about gas mileage—now, that ain't manly, and it got under my skin. I was racing motocross on my 400 Husqvarna, hauling it to the track with a trailer hitched to my Vette. One Sunday, after unloading the Husky, I had a 5-gallon can of gas. The old landlord didn't want gas stored in the basement (thanks to Kenny), and last time I left the can out, some jerk stole it and left a thank-you note. So, I poured a gallon into my tank and noticed Tom's VW sitting there. I poured the rest into his tank. I wish I could say I'd planned the perfect joke, but it didn't hit me until two days later. I was just being a nice guy.

Tom was bragging about his mileage: "I drove all over and didn't use any gas!" That's when the epiphany hit me like a truck. The next afternoon, I bought more gas, filled his VW to the top, and poured the rest into my tank. I did this every other day for two weeks. Tom was ecstatic, calling the VW dealership to brag he'd gone over 500 miles on one gallon. They asked him to bring it in to check it out. They looked everywhere and couldn't figure out why it was getting 500 miles per gallon it was just an average VW. Tom came home, telling me how amazed they were and how they wanted to call the factory. He was so proud. I never told him anything—I just stopped adding gas. A week later, he was hopping mad, wanting to sue. He didn't know what they'd done to kill his beautiful gas mileage or why. He thought it was a conspiracy with Standard Oil. He tried to get a lawyer, but no one believed him. He was never happy with just 30 miles per gallon and started hating corporate America. When he joined the Socialist Party, Vickie and I found another place to live. I never told him the truth, so if you're out there, Tom, you've probably told that story a hundred times. We're even.

I'm sure I've changed a bunch of lives, some for good and some maybe not so good but for sure Steven McQueen changed mine.

Chapter10: Steve McQueen Changed My Life

I never thought about it until a few minutes ago: Steve McQueen was the catalyst that changed my life. Yeah, he's the reason I turned out like I did! It's all Steve's fault, that's the ticket, all his fault. I didn't want to be him; it's just that he did things I thought were cool. So many of his movies left an impression, things I saw him do that I wanted to do. *The Thomas Crown Affair* didn't make me want to be an art thief; it made me want to drive a dune buggy on wet sand and fly a sailplane. I later did both. Who can forget those wide-open, green rolling fields he rode through in *The Great Escape*? Jumping that fence in his attempt to escape, I dreamed of that. Hell, I even loved the part where he bounced that baseball against the wall in "the cooler"; he was cool. I'd sit at my desk, pitching a baseball up in the air and catching it, it helped me think. My mom told me it was a bad idea, that I'd hit myself in the head. I later found out what she meant. I think that's when she told me "You won't be young forever!"

It started with a movie that few people saw. I was visiting my parents in Richmond, Texas, probably smelling faintly of Harley motor oil and acrylic lacquer paint. My mom, bless her heart, told me to pick a movie to see, probably hoping I'd choose something wholesome like *Mary Poppins*. Instead, I picked *On Any Sunday*, knowing nothing about it except that Steve McQueen was in it. Motorcycle racing? Never crossed my mind. I'd been paying my way through college by chopping motorcycles, turning rusty relics into gleaming beasts, but racing? That was for lunatics with a death wish. My mom, ever the saint, didn't bat an eye at my choice. She was like that—never complained, even when I dragged her to *Last Tango in Paris* with its butter-soaked themes. scene wasn't upsetting, but having your mom sitting next to you watching it? Now *that's* upsetting. sometimes she treated my just like my dad and "danced". I swear, she just smiled through it, probably praying for my soul. But I digress.

On Any Sunday hit me like a rogue spark plug to the skull. McQueen tearing through dirt tracks, deserts, and sand-duned beaches, kicking up clouds grinning like he'd just robbed a bank and gotten away with it—that was pure, unfiltered freedom. By the time the credits rolled, I was a goner. I bought the soundtrack the next day, blaring it on my beat-up 8-track stereo until the neighbors started throwing empty beer cans at my apartment. Then, in a move that still makes me wince, I sold my 1956 Panhead Harley—my pride and joy, with chrome that shone like a Texas sunset—and bought a brand-new 400cc Husqvarna motocross bike. That thing was a beast, all snarling power and no manners, like a bull with a two-stroke engine. The best way to describe it? Savage and anger. I ran on gas and adrenaline,

I called up Bill Haas, an old high school buddy who owned the motocross track in El Paso. Bill was the kind of guy who'd crash his bike, break three ribs, and still show up at the bar that night with a grin and a limp. When Bill entered the room, he sucked up all the oxygen. "You're late to the party, man," he said when I told him I was getting into racing. "But hell, better late than never." He introduced me to the motocross crowd—a wild mix of adrenaline junkies, gearheads, and guys who looked like they'd been chewed up by the track and spit out still smiling. There was Joel "Skidmark" Wolfson, who swore his lucky socks were the key to his wins (nobody dared ask when they'd last been washed or when he last won a race), and Annie Davis, who owned a Suzuki dealership, and her husband Don, who had a deal: if she won, she'd be on top; if he won, he'd be on top. They raced for sexual positions, so they never lost. Then there was good ol' Steven Nealy, who loved his 400cc Maico motocross bike so much he slept with it in his bedroom. He kept a cookie sheet under it at night, Maicos weren't housebroken.

My first day at the track was a comedy of errors. I showed up in jeans and a T-shirt, thinking I was Steve McQueen reincarnated, only to eat dirt on the first jump. Bill laughed so hard he nearly fell off his bike. "Kid, if you ride with your pants down, you're gonna get fucked!" But I was hooked. The roar of the engine, the sting of dirt in my eyes, the smell of castor oil, the sheer insanity of flying over a jump at 60 miles an hour—it was better than any movie, even *The Great Escape*. Being a motorcycle racer is like being in a fraternity: everybody's your bullshitting brother, but when the green flag drops, the bullshit stops. I just want to tell some of the stories. You ever seen a Navajo dreamcatcher? It's hung above the bed, catching bad dreams and negative energies in its web, letting only good dreams slide down the feathers to the sleeper. The bad dreams get trapped and burned away by morning sunlight. In racing, where bullshit is celebrated and encouraged, everything is captured and stored for later telling. Racing is 60% racing and 40% telling the "tall tales."

Take Steven Nealy and his beloved 400cc Maico. One day, I asked if I could ride it just once around the track. As a salesman, I finally talked him into it, but I had to let him hold my fake Rolex as collateral. He handed me the handlebars. I rode over a small hill, pulled to the side of the track, revved the engine to redline, and abruptly hit the kill switch. The engine screamed, then quit. I leaned the bike against a tree, then limped back over the hill with an exaggerated hobble. Steven was sure I'd totaled his bike and came charging at me, cursing and spitting rage, tears in his eyes. I told him I'd pay for half the repairs. Then he saw it, his Maico, pristine as ever, leaning against the tree. It's strange to see a grown man hug a motorcycle but hug it he did. Then he turned his attention to me. Luckily, I could outrun him on foot or on my bike.

Years later, when I thought he'd forgotten, I owned a General Motors dealership in Fort Stockton, Texas, and Steven came to visit, staying at my house. He considered himself a world-class chef and gave me some chocolate chip cookies he'd baked. They were great—until I started feeling and acting very strangely at my dealership. I found out later he'd laced them with grass. Oh well, fair's fair.

Next is a tale of two motocross racers on one bike.

Chapter 11: The Mexican American International Motocross Championship: A Dusty, Glorious Mess

Back in my wilder days, I dove headfirst into the gritty, adrenaline-fueled world of motocross, not just racing but helping orchestrate the chaos at Bill Haas's Borderland Motocross Park in El Paso. Picture me, covered in dirt, wrench in one hand, beer in the other, running races like a maestro of madness. One day, fate threw us a curveball when we met some high-rolling dudes from Juarez—fancy outfits, fancier bikes, and wallets that screamed "probably drug dealers." But they loved motocross, and that's what mattered. Over a few too many cervezas, we hatched a plan for the Mexican American International Motocross Championship (MAIMC), a cross-border showdown that'd make history—or at least a damn good bar story.

The deal was simple: first, a race in El Paso, where the top 10 riders from each class—five from the U.S., five from Mexico—would earn a golden ticket to the finals in Juarez. I tore up the El Paso track like a man possessed, snagging second place and a spot in the finals. The Juarez track? Oh, it was something else. They carved it out of what looked like a gravel pit abandoned by the gods. The terrain was so rough it sandblasted the paint off the Mexican riders' bikes and pitted their faces like the moon from years of eating dust. Uphills steeper than my ex's attitude, cliffs you'd only jump if you were crazy or drunk (I was both), and no fancy fences—just surveyor tape flapping in the wind, mocking us.

El Paso drew a respectable crowd of about a thousand fans, cheering and chugging. But Juarez? That was a whole different beast. Over 10,000 people showed up, a sea of screaming, flag-waving lunatics, with two national TV networks filming the spectacle. Vendors lined the pit, hawking motocross piñatas (imagine whacking a papier-mâché dirt bike for candy), ice-cold beers, and, well, some "extra entertainment" for those with looser morals. This wasn't just a race; it was a borderland circus.

My buddy David Berryhill got roped into being the flagman, probably because he owed someone a favor. Meanwhile, my pal Joel Wolfson rolled up on his 360 Yamaha DT, a street-legal relic that was less "motocross bike" and more "two-wheeled identity crisis." It had turn signals, a headlight, a taillight, and an ignition key dangling below the gas tank like it was ready to commute to work after the race. As we lined up at the start, engines roaring like a pack of angry lions, we revved hard—because that's what real motocross racers do. You couldn't hear a damn thing over the cacophony, which is probably why Joel didn't notice me lean over and flip his ignition key to off. There he was, twisting the throttle like a madman, revving an engine deader than disco, completely oblivious.

Then came the start, and oh, what a start. Berryhill, our fearless flagman, strutted out like he owned the place, ready to wave the green flag. Except someone—probably a drunk fan or a rival's cousin, had swiped it. Undeterred, Berryhill yanked off his bright red toupee with the flair of a magician pulling a rabbit from a hat. He dropped it to the ground like a sacred ritual, then hoisted it high, waving it like the checkered flag of a fever dream. Half the field froze, probably thinking, "Is this in the rulebook?" Spoiler: it was. Page 47, Section 3: "In case of flag theft, a vibrant toupee may be substituted to commence an international championship."

I shot off the line like a bullet, tires spitting gravel, while Joel sat there revving his silent bike, probably wondering if he'd forgotten to pay his engine's electric bill. The other half of the field, still confused by the toupee fiasco, lagged behind. The track was a beast—berms that launched you into orbit, cliffs that dared you to fly, and surveyor tape that seemed to whisper, "Good luck, idiot." On the white flag lap (the last one, for you newbies), I was still in second, but man, I was beat. Might've been the beers I'd chugged between motos—hydration is key, right? Then disaster struck. I misjudged a berm, slid out, and vanished into the crowd like a rock star stage-diving into a mosh pit.

I was wearing my old drag racing jersey from Juarez—Santiago Martinez and Sons Racing Team across the top, Jaimie Guerra Driver across the bottom. The locals must've thought I was one of their own, because they went into full hero mode. Hands grabbed my bike, hoisted me up, and lifted the surveyor tape like it was the velvet rope at a VIP club. I roared back onto the track, still in second place, but something felt off. I glanced back—no rival racers, just a 10-year-old kid clinging to me like a human backpack, grinning ear to ear. How he got there, I'll never know. Maybe he saw his chance for glory and hitched a ride.

With the finish line in sight, I gunned the Husky, 400, and we—me and my pint-sized stowaway, flew through the air on slow motion, like a low-budget action movie. We crossed the line, securing second place in a cloud of dust and cheers. At the trophy presentation, I called the kid up to the podium. I handed him the trophy, a shiny testament to our accidental partnership, and the crowd lost their minds, roaring like we'd just won the World Cup. Joel, meanwhile, was still back at the start, probably cursing his key. Berryhill was busy reattaching his toupee, claiming it was "aerodynamic." And me? I was just happy to survive the wildest race on that side of the Rio Grande, with a story—and a kid—that'd go down in motocross legend.

Speaking of legends, El Paso's own Albert Jones of Jones Harley Davidson and our wacky friendship.

Chapter 12: The Knock, Knock, Knock Story

El Paso, Texas, isn't just a dot on the map where the Old West supposedly hung up its spurs. No, sir, it's a place where the spirit of those rowdy, dust-kicking days lives on, fueled by something in the water—folks say it's the lithium, but it might just be pure, unfiltered Texan grit. The people of El Paso? They're a breed apart, a tribe of their own, standing tall and proud, different even from other Texans. You can hear it in the air, thick with their Western porch twang laced with Mexican cadence, spinning analogies so colorful they'd make a city slicker's head spin. These folks don't just talk; they weave tales as wild as the Chihuahuan Desert wind. I was thinking about Albert Jones the other day, a man who was as much a legend as the Harleys he sold, and I figured his story's one that needs telling because El Paso isn't El Paso without him.

In the heart of this sunbaked city during the 1960s, on a gritty stretch of Texas Street where tumbleweeds might've rolled if the pavement hadn't been so cracked, stood Albert Jones' Harley-Davidson, a two-story brick building that looked like it had seen better days, probably back when Billy the Kid was still causing trouble. The ground floor was the dealership, a shrine to chrome and horsepower, with a wooden showroom floor so soaked in Harley oil it could've fueled a small rebellion. Upstairs was an apartment, reachable only by a rickety ladder since the stairs had given up the ghost years ago, too worn out to argue with gravity. The back room was the shop and parts department, cramped but functional, with space for maybe five bikes if you didn't mind being cozy. Out in the parking lot, Albert kept his pride and joy: a Harley drag bike he called the "222," a monstrous beast that three Panhead 74 engines lined up like cannons in a row. He'd fire it up with an 18-wheeler impact gun, claiming it could rip through a quarter mile in six seconds at 180 mph. The older Albert got, the faster that bike seemed to go in his stories, and nobody dared call him on it.

Now, Albert was tougher than the back end of a shooting gallery. A former motorcycle cop,

He'd seen every trick in the book and had a stare that could make a rattlesnake think twice. Smart folks knew better than to cross him. Me? I wasn't in that category. I was a young, dumb kid with a knack for trouble and a love for Harleys, and for reasons I'll never fully understand, Albert took a shine to me. Maybe I reminded him of some other fool he'd known back in the day. He had a stockpile of old parts and older wisdom, both of which I helped myself to, sometimes with permission, sometimes with a five-finger discount. Albert wasn't blind to my antics. He'd tell his mechanic, Red, to weigh me before I left the shop, knowing Harley parts weren't featherlight. It was a game to him, catching me red-handed, and he played it with a grin hidden behind that ever-present stogie he chewed but never lit.

One dusty afternoon, I was poking around the dealership when my eyes landed on a sorry sight: a 1954 Panhead, or what was left of it. Someone had tried to chop it into a custom ride but gave up halfway, leaving it with a hacked-off rear fender, no seat, and an oil leak that was more like a river. Back then, chopper parts weren't something you could just order from a catalog.

Whoever started this project had enthusiasm but not much else, just a claw hammer and a hacksaw, by the looks of it. Albert was in his office, pretending to read the *El Paso Herald*, one eye peeking over the paper, that unlit stogie rolling from one side of his Albert was in his office, pretending to read the *El Paso Herald*, one eye peeking over the paper, that unlit stogie rolling from one side of his mouth to the other. "Warr, what the hell are you doing?" he hollered, his voice booming like a shotgun blast.

I shot back, "Trying to figure out why you'd let this piece of shit sit on your showroom floor next to all these fine Hogs!" Albert had no love for choppers or the long-haired types who rode them. His taste ran to his 1965 Panhead, decked out with so many lights it looked like he was riding a Christmas tree at night, a glowing testament to his flair for the dramatic. He smirked and said, "I put that thing there just for you, kid."

I told him I was flat broke, and even if I had cash, I wouldn't waste it on that heap. "What you got to trade, then?" he asked, leaning back in his chair. Now, I did have a 1959 VW Bug, which I'd planned to turn into a dune buggy until I started it one day and heard a "knock, knock, knock" that sounded like the engine was begging for mercy. Rod knock, but instead of telling Albert that, I grinned and said, "I got a '59 VW Bug I'd trade."

Albert raised an eyebrow. "Will it make it here?" he asked. I nodded. I just didn't tell him how. "If it gets here, we'll swap even-steven," he said, then added, "That Panhead's got a leaky petcock, so I can't fill it with gas, but I'll throw in a new one for the trade."

I hightailed it home and called my buddy Ken Chamberlain. "Bring your trailer," I said. "We're towing the Bug to Texas Street." The plan was simple but devious: we'd unload the Bug a few blocks from Jones Harley-Davidson, take the trailer off the truck, then use the truck to push the VW down Texas Street at about 45 miles an hour. I coasted into the parking lot, smooth as a conman's smile, right as Albert was chatting with a customer. I hopped out, tossed him the keys, and said, "She's all yours." Albert just nodded, stogie bobbing. "Meet me inside in a few minutes to sign the titles. Go load up your bike." I knew what I was doing; I just didn't know what I was thinking.

Ken and I loaded the Panhead onto the trailer, laughing so hard we could barely breathe. Back at my place, I installed the new petcock, and Ken dumped a gallon of lawnmower gas into the tank. I gave the Harley a kick, and it roared to life—then came the sound: "knock, knock, knock." Same damn noise as the Bug. I killed the engine, heart sinking, just as my mom poked her head into the garage. "Alberts on the phone," she said.

I knew I was in for it. Youth makes you bold, but it doesn't always make you smart. I picked up the phone, said, "Hello," and Albert's laughter hit me like a freight train before he even spoke. That's when I learned what irony really means. When he finally caught his breath, he growled, "Warr, get your sorry ass down here." At 6 foot 5 and 240 pounds, I wasn't scared of a fight, but getting chewed out by Albert? That was another story. Ken, the coward, refused to come along.

When I pulled up to the dealership, Albert was in his office with two motorcycle cops, all of them grinning like they'd just heard the punchline of the century. He'd been telling them what would soon be known across El Paso as the "Knock, Knock, Knock Story." I braced for handcuffs, but Albert pointed at me with that stogie and said, "There's the kid responsible, right there." The cops, old buddies of his, burst out laughing. They shook my hand, told Albert they never thought they'd see the day he got outfoxed, and made me retell the story right there. From then on, every time an El Paso motorcycle cop pulled me over, they'd see my name, ask if I was the "Knock, Knock, Knock" guy, and make me recount the tale before letting me go with a chuckle.

Albert, ever the stoic, took it in stride. "We both got what we deserved," he said, and he meant it. He knew my folks were about to move to Dallas, leaving me without a place to crash. He opened a closet door in his office, rolled that stogie across his mouth, and said, "Follow me." He led me to a ladder—like I said, the only way up to that second-floor apartment, since the stairs had long since surrendered. Up there was a fully furnished place, frozen in time, the furniture trapped because no one could get it down. "Warr, you can stay here till you find a place," he said. It was a kind gesture from a man who didn't have to care but did anyway.

Years later, Albert sold the dealership to Sherman Barnett, who turned it into the biggest Harley-Davidson dealership in the world. Albert, too stubborn to retire, stayed on in the parts department. Sherman, unlike Albert, had no patience for my rummaging ways, but Albert and I stayed friends until the day he passed. He was what West Texans call a "good ol' boy," the kind of man who could outsmart you, outtalk you, and still make you feel like you'd won something just by knowing him. And in El Paso, where the Old West never really died, Albert Jones was proof that the real legends are the people, not the place.

Chapter 13: The Terlingua Flash and Velvet Jones

Desert racers are an eclectic bunch; gnarly would be a good word to describe them. Every year, we'd pile into trucks and head to the wild, dusty heart of Terlingua for the legendary Terlingua Enduro, hosted on a sprawling, sunscorched ranch owned by a grizzled old Rancher named Pepper, whose land lay just west of the majestic Big Bend National Park. Pepper has what you would call a western drawl. I once introduced him to a friend of mine from New York Saul

Faultfinder who flew in to race the Terlingua Enduro. It was funny because neither one could understand a word the other one said. Pepper asks Saul "Whereabout's are fromboy, you from England?" Saul looked at me with a quizzical look.

So, I said in my perfect speech, "Where are you from son?' I left off the part about England. He responded white looking at me with "Yo, I'm from B'klyn, fuhgeddaboudit! I turned to Pepper who was looking at me and waiting for a translation. "He's from Brooklin." The conversation went one for a few minutes with each one waiting for my translation which was strange… we were all speaking English. Saul and Pepper became good friends; they weren't brought together by a common language but by a common love of Cazadores Tequela of which Saul had an endless supply of. "All weekend, Pepper would haul his West Texas compadres over an' say, 'Y'all listen to my ol' buddy Saul jaw a spell.' "Then tell me what he's saying. "fuhgeddaboudit
The Terlingua Enduro was 125 miles of cow trails and dry creek beds. This adrenaline-pumping race, set against a backdrop of rugged desert canyons and towering, copper-hued mesas, creeks using their steam shovel power endless time to carve canyons into granite. It magically

attracted a wild and crazy roaring crowd of 600 riders, their bikes kicking up clouds of red earth under the endless Texas sky where if a Giant Cumulus Cloud didn't top out at over 50,000 feet it was called a puff. The stars at night are so close you can point them out with a flashlight. I don't know how Pepper was able to entice them to come so close. Right alongside the iconic Terlingua Chili Cook-Off, held on the same weathered patch of Pepper's ranch, it was the grandest spectacle in the Big Bend region—a vibrant, raucous drunk celebration of speed, spice, and untamed frontier spirit with its eclectic share of millionaires and prostitutes, pasters, drug smugglers Banditos and Desert Racers.

One year I loaded my motorhome with some of my friends, Al Tocterman; a Midland Oilman, TT Larose; a train engineer, Rick Aaron, I don't know what he did for a living, David Berryhill occupation unknown. We were men, we didn't talk about shit like that. My LB (Lovely Bride) Vickie made us a huge pot of her world-famous spaghetti. She told me all I had to do was heat it up and serve it. We actually had a cage of Coors which would make us very popular at the race. I was the designated driver because I don't drink. We damn near starved that first night; Vickie never told me that before I heated it, I should add water. That's the night I came up with the now famous treat; Burn-baked spaghetti. Both Berryhill and Pepper's goats seem to like it.

The way an enduro works is it's a timed event and they start four people at a time every minute starting at 8:00 AM. Now Rick Aaron is a peculiar fellow. He took an old 54 Studebaker pickup and put a 500 cubic inch Cadilac motor in it the he painted satin black. He raced an old 250 Suzuki which he also painted satin black… everything on it was satin black, the spokes on his wheels, the chrome handlebars, everything. He raced in a pair of black long sleave overalls, even his gas can was satin black.

He was the first one of us to start and when he had 2 minutes before it was his turn he reached into his pocket and pulled on a pint of Black Velvet Whisky, twisted the cap off and chugalugged the entire bottle then he placed his hand under his arm pit and shouted "NIT, NIT, NIT! And through the bottle in a dry creek where it shattered into a million pieces. After this show no one else on his minute or anyone behind him wanted to get close to him. We all knew the truth, and I know I almost fell off my bike laughing so hard; it wasn't whisky, it was watered down coke. From that day till today everyone calls him "The Black Velvet".

TT LaRose was a great guy, he was at every race, all decked out in his leathers and shiny helmet but for all the years that we knew him he never raced. When asked, "TT, are you racing pro or amateur today?" He would reply, "I only dress this way to pick up girls." Come to think about that wasn't a bad Idea even though racing motorcycles was the best way I know to meet nurses, there are plenty of unattached girls in the pits when the men were racing and there isn't any need for stitches.

David Berryhill was a friend of mine; he lived in the oil fields just north of Imperial TX. His girlfriend that everybody called "Fud" was later on be the poster child for every waitress in Austin; she was covered with tats from her head to her toes. The first time I met David he had a colonel's Army Delta Force uniform hanging behind the seat of his 56 International pickup. He told me that he had a mental breakdown in The Grenada War, and they gave him a medical discharge. I assumed he was telling the truth because it was obvious he was "As goofy as a football bat."

He liked to race dressed in what he called "Commando Gear", full desert camo. Until that day I didn't realize he had a different definition of "Going Commando", he didn't wear any underwear. Normally this subject would never come up but in that 125-mile race you must re-fuel about two times. Now David was a dandy; he lived in a single wide 1950-style mobile home. He had better tires on the roof than on his 56 International pickups, he didn't have a washer or a dryer and the Pecos River that ran 10 feet from his front door tasted like the Russian Army had all sneezed in it. What I am trying to say is he's leather stank' really bad! Well, the day of the race at somewhere near mile 70 David hit a pucker bush and did what we call a "Flying W". That's where both his feet came off the pegs and went straight up into the air, spread wide. Thus, the flying W. That move was more than those rotten leathers could take, and they split from one knee to the next. Remember he was riding "Commando". One thing you never do when you're riding an Enduro is quit, only sissies quit but he needed to pull into the pit and get some gas. Remember that's where all the girlfriends are.

The pit was in a little valley next to a stream. They put it there so the wives and kids could play in that crystal clear water while the waited. David had to make a choice; it was a conundrum. No matter what he did, quit or go on he needed gas. So, he squeezed his legs together as tight as he could, for the first time in his life he felt lucky he wasn't very well endowed, which would be demonstrated very soon.

There it sat, his five-gallon gas tank, all by itself. He cautiously pulls up to it but he knew that if he got off his motorcycle and filled up his tank all those women and kids would see his "Johnson". He tried to get someone's attention, but everyone was busy, so he put two fingers in his mouth and whistled. I sounded like a steam whistle, loud and shrill. That got a lot more attention than he wanted. Two guys and three women came over to investigate. "Ladies I had an accident, and I don't want to cause a scene so would you three women be so kind as to avert their eyes while one of you gentlemen would please poor some gas into my tank. This didn't go smoothly; the men call some more people over and the women pointed and laughed. David had a good grip on the situation with both hands. He had killed the bike without a thought of how he was going to be able to stand up, and kick start it again with a hundred eyes on him.

When the guy took David gas cap off and lifted the gas can up high to poor it in the gas tank, the nozzle came off. It dumped 5 gallons of gas in Davids exposed crotch. The pain must have been extreme; I've never had 5 gallons of gas dumped on my crotch so I would know but Berryhill claims it's excruciating. He forgot about all decency and screamed like his balls were on fire as he jumped off or a better word would be "Fell off" and the scrambled to his feet and ran as fast as a man can with his balls on fire to the creek screaming the whole way.

As he sat in that cooling water Pepper walked up and ask him if he wanted a light? Everybody was laughing at his pain but finally Pepper loaded David's bike into the back of his truck and took him back to camp. That day will live in infamy and David would from that day forward be known as the "Terlingua Flash"!

Terlingua is famous for its Chilli Cook Off, but Fabens Texas has its own Frijoles Gas Off. Their logo is a blue flame.

Chapter 14: The Great Frijoles Fiesta Fiasco

Henry Giagos, a man with a mustache so grand it could star in its own Western, was the president of the Fabens Jaycees, while I, a self-proclaimed tequila aficionado with questionable decision-making skills, led the Fort Stockton Jaycees. The Jaycees were a national outfit for young men aged 18 to 35, preaching that "service to humanity is the greatest work of life." Let's be real, though—it was a fraternity for guys who never outgrew their frat-boy phase, an excuse to ditch town, drink with buddies, and call it "community service."

When Henry called to invite us to the Fabens Frijoles Cook-Off, which his club was sponsoring, his voice crackled with enthusiasm, like a man who'd already sampled the beans. "Come on down, amigos! Bring your best frijoles recipe!" he bellowed. I had a recipe: open a can of beans, pour into a pot, cook, then pour cornbread mix on top and cook some more. Every heaping spoonful delivered delicious cornbread and beans. I had visions of being the "National Champion." I rallied the Fort Stockton JCs at our usual haunt, the back room of Sara's Cafe, to brainstorm. They thought cooking beans was too much work. Tom Miller, our resident idea guy with a mullet that begged for respect and screamed 1984, had a better plan. "Forget beans. Let's haul our old saloon front, pour free tequila, and let folks fire a 12-gauge shotgun after three shots. It's foolproof!" I pointed out the obvious—mixing booze and firearms was a one-way ticket to the ER. Enter Jim Eastup, our slick insurance salesman with a smile that could sell flood coverage for a swimming pool. "No worries, boss," Jim winked, twirling a pen like a gunslinger. "I'll pop open the shells and dump the pellets. Safe as a church picnic!"

What could possibly go wrong?

Fabens, Texas, is 90% Hispanic, and our only Hispanic member, Oscar Renteria, was dubbed our "translator." Problem was, Oscar's Spanish was limited to "taco" and "cerveza," despite looking like he'd stepped out of a Home Depot parking lot. "I got the vibe, man," Oscar shrugged, adjusting his cowboy hat to hide his panic. "I'll just nod and smile."

As a tequila connoisseur—self-certified after a weekend in Juarez—I splurged on a case of Cazadores Tequila, the good stuff from Arandas, Jalisco. Founded in 1922 by José María Bañuelos, Cazadores uses a fancy 24-step diffusion process to squeeze 99% of the juice from raw agave, no cooking needed. Their yeast ferments to Mozart's tunes, making it smoother than a lounge singer but with a kick like a mule with a grudge. I figured it'd class up our saloon stunt. We rolled into Fabens, set up our rickety saloon front—complete with swinging doors that squeaked like a horror movie—and I kicked things off with a bang. Literally. Six shots of Cazadores and two 12-gauge blasts into the sky later, I was feeling like Pancho Villa at a fiesta. The crowd swarmed, drawn by free booze and the chance to play cowboy. Fabens folks, already hyped on frijoles and mariachi, turned our booth into the hottest spot at the cook-off. People lined up, grinning like kids at a piñata party, ready for their three shots and a trigger pull. Young and old, the Jaycees cajoled every pretty woman to give it a try. I tell you right now, if you want a crowd bigger than the World Cup, have a bunch of scantily clad, intoxicated women shoot a 12-gauge shotgun in the air. The lines to watch put Disneyland to shame.

We took turns bartending, passing the Cazadores like it was holy water. Doug and Deby, the power couple who ran Fort Stockton's Western Auto, were behind the bar when trouble strolled up in a Budweiser shirt. The Bud truck driver, a burly guy with a beard that looked like it housed small animals and a chest like a barrel, pounded three shots, fired his shotgun blast from the hip, and demanded more. "Three more, let's go!" he slurred, swaying like a piñata in a windstorm. He did three more, set the shotgun butt on top of his head, and wanted to go for nine. Doug consulted our "Safety and Dispute Manager," Clyde Sawyer, another insurance man who'd seen it all. Clyde, three shots deep himself, waved him off. "Six is plenty, pal. We'll run out of tequila before we run out of fools like you!" Wise words, but the tequila was doing the talking.

The Bud driver wasn't having it. In a move that'd make a soap opera blush, he lunged across the bar for the bottle, missing it entirely and grabbing a handful of Deby's, ahem, prominently displayed assets (Bodacious Tatas). Deby, a firecracker with a wardrobe that left little to the imagination, shrieked, "Hands off the merchandise, you drunk sasquatch!" Doug, a man who'd wrestle a bear for his wife, vaulted the bar like an Olympic hurdler and tackled the guy. A cloud of dust erupted, with fists, boots, and elbows flying. Then, holy frijoles, I saw it—Doug bit off the dude's right ear! He looked up, flashed a bloody grin, and spit it into the dirt like a deranged pit bull. I dove for the ear, but every time I got close, a stray kick sent it skittering like a hockey puck in a bar fight.

The crowd was in chaos, half cheering, half yelling in Spanish. Oscar, our "translator," was hiding by the taco stand, pretending to be a local. "I'm just here for the food, man," he muttered, shoving a taco in his face. The sheriff rolled up, lights flashing, and everyone started jabbering in Spanish. I grabbed Oscar, who panicked and blurted, "¡Eha, araba!" Useless. Fearing a night in the clink, we tore down our saloon like a NASCAR pit crew and hightailed it back to Fort Stockton, leaving a trail of dust and bad decisions.

I called Henry the next day, and he filled me in, laughing so hard he nearly choked on his coffee. The Bud driver, too drunk to find his remaining ear, stumbled around looking for the one Doug turned into a chew toy. His buddy, the

Coke truck driver, tried to play hero, taking his keys to drive him to the hospital. But those two geniuses got into their own brawl and flipped the Coke truck into a cotton field. Blood, soda cans, and regrets everywhere. The Highway Patrol showed up to quell a "riot," finding the Bud and Coke drivers still slugging it out like a low-budget boxing match.

Both were arrested, but the Coke driver talked his way out. The Bud driver wasn't so lucky. A reporter for the *El Paso Times* at the cook-off snapped him chugging tequila in his Budweiser shirt, and the next morning, his mug was plastered on the front page with the headline, "Local Man Loses Ear, Dignity at Frijoles Fiesta." His wife, waiting at the hospital, served him divorce papers as he came out of surgery, forcing him to hear the bad news through his one good ear. An hour later, his boss called and fired him. Handcuffed to his hospital bed, he faced charges for assault, public fighting, drunk and disorderly, and "assorted shenanigans," as Henry put it.

Back in Fort Stockton, the JCs held an emergency meeting to dissect our glorious failure. Tom, still proud of his saloon idea, suggested, "Next time, two shots max. And Deby, maybe wear a turtleneck." Deby, polishing a new shotgun shell necklace she'd made as a trophy, shot back, "Or maybe you boys learn to aim your fists better." We all agreed: the tequila was the real MVP, and we'd probably do it again—just with better translators and fewer ears on the menu. From then on, every party we threw came with a clear rule, stated plain as day: "No Ears!"

Next meet Linda, a woman that always makes me laugh.

Chapter 15: Celery

Bruce, my good friend and neighbor in El Paso, ran a used car dealership next to a 7-11 that reeked of burnt nachos and dreams of a better Slurpee. He could sell a skateboard to a snake, his grin promising, "Trust me, this'll be fun." His laugh roared like a V8 engine, and he tossed "pard" into every sentence, making you feel like his co-star in a buddy-cop flick. His wife, Linda, was a stunner—five-foot-six, with blond hair that caught the light like polished gold and blue eyes that sparkled with wit. She wasn't just a looker; she was the heart of the lot, her warmth and quick humor making customers feel like they were picking out a car with their favorite cousin. In the car business, playful jabs were currency, and Bruce and Linda traded them like poker chips. Picture Bruce hyping a beat-up sedan—"This baby's got character!"—while Linda, with a playful eye roll, chimed in, "Yeah, character that sings karaoke at 2 a.m." The mechanics, Hank and Billy (Linda's brother), doubled over, their coffee-stained grins lighting up the lot. Once, wiry Hank, with a laugh like a backfiring muffler, bet a case of Dr Pepper that Linda couldn't outsell Bruce on a Saturday. "Seven cars, Linda? You're dreaming!" Bruce teased. "Watch me, pard—I'll have you polishing my heels by sundown," she shot back. She moved seven cars to his five, then blasted "Sweet Home Alabama" on the lot's ancient PA, twirling like a kid in a sprinkler.

As a used car wholesaler, I was pitching Bruce a deal when Linda announced she was thirsty and heading to the 7-11 for a Big Gulp. "Anybody else want something?" she asked. Bruce wanted a Cherry Coke "big enough to drown a rattlesnake," Hank craved a Mountain Dew "to keep my gears grinding," Billy begged for a Dr Pepper "ice-cold as my ex's heart," and Jimmy, the salesman reeking of Old Spice, demanded a root beer "with extra fizz, like my personality." Linda jotted it down with a smirk, her pen moving like she was signing a million-dollar deal, then asked me to help carry the drinks.

Linda was dressed to kill in a black bodycon dress, tight and stretchy, paired with Prada heels flashing their signature red soles. Her sun-kissed hair cascaded over her shoulders, and a faint lavender scent trailed her. She looked like Margot Robbie's twin, her feminine laugh filling the air with warmth. At the 7-11, two roughnecks—one tall and lanky, the other short in a flat-brimmed cowboy hat like a thumbtack—loitered up front, their eyes glued to her. I grabbed some beef jerky while Linda headed to the drink station. She sensed their lewd stares, a whiff of vulgarity in the air. I stepped up. "What're you two looking at?" The tall one sneered, "Well, duh!" I leaned in, deadpan, and said, "I don't know what you boys are into, but that's a guy." The thumbtack scoffed, "Bullshit!" with a Texan twang. "Fella, I'd stake my truck on her being a woman." I shrugged. "Your call, but that's your business." Doubt flickered in their eyes. The tall one muttered, "If that's a guy... I must be gay."

Back at the drink station, I whispered to Linda, "Two guys up front are ogling you. I told 'em you're a guy." She grinned, used to the attention and loving the game. At the counter, she set down the drinks and boomed in a deep, masculine voice, "Do you sell condoms here?"

The roughnecks froze, then bolted, playfully punching each other outside. Linda's laugh rang out like a jukebox hitting the perfect song. "Those boys'll tell that story at every honky-tonk from here to Lubbock," she whispered, tossing me a wink.

Two weeks later, I gave Linda a ride to the Bombay Bicycle Club south of Bassett Center to pick up a car. With time to kill, we grabbed drinks at the bar. Linda looked sharp in a sleek gray business suit, her short skirt accentuating her confident stride, a subtle perfume lingering. The club buzzed with wealthy Mexicans in $2,500 Armani suits and diamond pinky rings. As Linda climbed onto a tall bar stool, one hip at a time, showing a flash of leg, the room froze—the jukebox seemed to skip. Every head turned, even the woman bartender's eyes bulging like a cartoon wolf.

"Does it bother you?" I asked. She smirked. "If it bothered me, I'd wear a longer skirt. Wanna see something funny?" I nodded, already chuckling at her mischief. She ordered a Bloody Mary with a celery stick. Her red fingernails gleamed as she slowly pulled the celery out, tomato juice dripping, then slid it back in. "Watch the room," she said. She parted her lips, licking the juice from the bottom up, building intensity with each pass. The crowd was spellbound, their fancy suits forgotten. I'm six-foot-five, 240 pounds—nobody messed with us, but Linda didn't need me. She owned the room.

"Get ready for the finale," she whispered, dipping the celery again, juice coating her fingers. She slid the whole stalk into her mouth, red lipstick gleaming, sucking every drop with a soft moan. Then, with a seductive pout, she bared her pearly teeth and bit the tip off. Every man crossed their legs in unison, like a dance team. We burst out laughing. Linda was all feminine, but her laughter was more like you'd expect from a female bear. "I don't care who you are, that's funny," I said. A jealous wife at a nearby table shot Linda a glare, muttering to her husband, who just adjusted his $5,000 Berluti loafers. The bartender, still dazed, comped her drink, stammering, "Lady, you're worth every penny."

My gift of gab is a tool I use to get what I want. Linda's gift—her charm, her flair—was hers, honed on the lot with Bruce's laugh echoing in the background. It was just life: skills you wield to make every day louder, brighter, and a little more fun.

Next met Beowulf's nemesis Grindel.

Chapter 16: Grindel

Let me tell you about Grendel, my cantankerous Harley Sportster, a bike with a personality as cooperative as a skunked cat at bath time. Starting that beast was like solving a Rubik's Cube blindfolded. Grendel had a Tillotson carburetor, which, unlike your average bike, didn't sip gas politely when you twisted the throttle—it squirted it into the cylinders like a kid with a Super Soaker. Twist too much, and you'd flood the engine faster than you could say "kickstart knee lock." My routine was sacred: one throttle twist, hold it open, then kick like you're auditioning for a ninja movie. It worked every time. Deviate from the script, though, and Grendel would sulk, leaving you cursing and sweating. That bike had rules and ignoring them was like challenging a grumpy old wizard to a duel.

I'm a motorcycle junkie, plain and simple. My son Casey, a guitar-slinging dreamer, once said no true guitarist stops buying axes until they can't stash any more under the bed. That's me with bikes. I'd have kept Grendel and his two-wheeled cousins forever, but my garage was starting to look like a chopper museum, and my wife, Vickie—bless her practical soul—drew the line at storing them in the kitchen. "It's a stupid idea," she said, rolling her eyes so hard I thought they'd spin out of her head. Women! I love her, but sometimes I think she speaks a different language, one where "vintage Harley" doesn't translate to "art." So, with a heavy heart, I decided Grendel needed a new home.

I owned a Chevrolet dealership in Fort Stockton, so I rolled Grendel into the showroom, where she gleamed under the lights like a rock star awaiting his encore. Enter Rodney, a wide-eyed young guy with dreams of cruising Dickerson Street, and his girlfriend, Cindy, a halter-topped vision who looked like she stepped out of a Beach Boys song. The moment Rodney laid eyes on

Grendel, it was love at first sight. I could see it in his face—he was already picturing himself and Cindy roaring through town, turning heads like a Hollywood power couple. The deal was as good as done; we just needed to dot the i's and rev the engine.

Rodney was itching for a test ride, so I gave him the Grendel Gospel: "Twist the throttle once, then hold it open. No more, no less." He nodded, but his eyes were glazed with excitement, like a kid on Christmas morning after an adrenaline shot. I started Grendel for him, and off they went, Cindy clinging to Rodney's waist, both grinning like they'd just won the lottery. I figured they'd be back in ten minutes, ready to sign the papers.

Twenty minutes later, I spotted them trudging back, pushing Grendel like a pair of sweaty, defeated pioneers. Rodney's hair was plastered to his forehead, and Cindy's halter top was looking more "marathon chic" than "biker babe." "Couldn't get the damn thing started!" Rodney panted, glaring at Grendel like it had personally insulted his mother. I felt a pang of guilt—I should've made sure he understood the bike's quirks. Clearly, he'd flooded the engine worse than a monsoon.

I sauntered over, grabbed the handlebars, and started chatting to buy time while I secretly worked my magic. As I talked, I eased the throttle open, letting fresh air clear out the fuel-soaked mess Rodney had made. "You ever owned a Harley before?" I asked. He shook his head, still catching his breath. "Well, son, there's secret Harley owners don't tell outsiders. A Harley ain't just a bike; it's a partner. You got to harmonize, like you're in a band. Curse it, and it'll curse you right back. Watch this."

I leaned in, caressing the bottom of Grendel's tank like it was a loyal old dog, and started crooning the theme from *Then Came Bronson*, that old TV show about a lone rider on a Sportster, drifting across America and fixing folks' problems. In my best lounge-singer impression, I purred, "Goin' down that long, lonesome highway, gonna live life my way…" All the while, the throttle was open, and Grendel's engine was quietly forgiving Rodney's sins. Cindy giggled, and Rodney looked at me like I'd lost my marbles, but I pressed on. "See? You got to bond. Show it some love."

I stepped back and nodded at Rodney. "Now, hold the throttle open and give it one good kick. Just one." He hesitated, then climbed on, looking like he was about to wrestle a bear. He jumped, slammed the kickstart, and—hallelujah!

Grendel roared to life, purring like a smug lion who'd outsmarted a zookeeper. The clouds didn't actually part, but it felt like they did.

Rodney's jaw dropped, Cindy squealed and planted a kiss on his cheek, and he turned to me with a grin. "We'll take it!" They rode off, and even from behind, I could tell they were beaming like kids on a carnival ride.

A week later, I bumped into the mailman, Carl, in the dealership hallway. He looked at me with bleary eyes, like he hadn't slept in days. "Did you sell Rodney that Harley?" he asked, sounding mildly accusing. I nodded, bracing for a complaint. "Well, he's gone nuts. I live next door, and my bedroom's right by his carport. Every morning, he's out there at dawn, singing some damn song about 'living life his way' and petting that bike like it's a puppy. Yesterday, I caught him whispering sweet nothings to the gas tank!"

I chuckled, picturing Rodney serenading Grendel under the carport lights. "Sounds like him and Grendel have bonded," I said. Carl shook his head, muttering about earplugs, but I couldn't help but smile. Grendel had found his match—a dreamer crazy enough to love her quirks. Somewhere out there, Grendel, Rodney, and Cindy were cruising Dickerson Street, harmonizing with that stubborn old Sportster, living life their way. And me? I was already eyeing a new bike to fill the Grindel-shaped hole in my garage. Vickie's gonna kill me.

Chapter 17: I Hate Him

Typically, I find great pleasure in recounting stories of practical jokes, the amusement evident in the smiles and laughter of my audience. On this occasion, my closest friend, Ken Chamberlin, took on the role of the mischievous instigator I usually play. The scene at Eagles Nest airfield south of Odessa/Midland was bustling with laughter, its vibrant echoes filling the air, as Ken played his prank with finesse, leaving me at the center of everyone's amusement. The airfield buzzed with anticipation, the scent of excitement mingling with the faint aroma of devious smiles and lingering laughter. The moment left everyone exhilarated and curious, eager to witness the unfolding of Ken's masterful trick. Ken and I spent countless hours soaring through the sky in our sailplanes, taking off from this familiar airport. The joke he played on me would've been uproariously hilarious if I'd pulled it on him. Visualizing his response brought a sparkle to my eye and a mischievous smile to my face. But Ken, bless his heart, wasn't as lighthearted as I was. He hated being the butt of a prank, especially one this clever. He'd never admit to falling for such a trick, his disbelief and embarrassment would've saturated the air with fury. Me? I could acknowledge the brilliance of his scheme. I hate him.

Ken was a General Motors dealer in Monahans, Texas, and I ran the Chevrolet dealership in Fort Stockton. We've been the closest friends since our days at Eastwood High School in El Paso, Texas. Our dealerships were about 45 minutes apart (in West Texas, distances are measured in time; 70 miles = 45 minutes when you're not in a hurry). We were fiercely competitive.

One hot July day, I gazed out my office window and saw the most stunning clouds I'd ever laid eyes on. To a sailplane pilot, enormous cumulus clouds with flat bottoms are a joy to behold—they signal rising air perfect for soaring. Sailplanes position themselves beneath those clouds, disconnect the tow rope, and circle in the updraft. I called Ken and told him to look out his window and describe what he saw. He went on about a girl with long legs in incredibly short shorts. I let him finish, then said, "Look higher." He still didn't get it, launching into an even better description of the girl. Finally, I told him to look at the sky. When he realized I was talking about cumulus nimbus clouds, not a girl in hot pants, he said, "I'll meet you at Eagles Nest in about 30 minutes" (70 miles when you're in a hurry in West Texas).

My trip to Eagles Nest was delayed by a Highway Patrol officer with no grasp of West Texas time (103 mph in a 55-mph zone). By the time I arrived, Ken was already in the air, but he couldn't find lift in a push-up bra. He was lining up to land, apparently thinking Eagles Nest was 150 feet higher than it was, because his approach was high and fast. I'm certain he pulled the flaps instead of the air brake, stalling three feet above the ground and touching down only when the wind subsided.

As the type of guy who always helps a friend and never embarrasses unless it's in public, I doubled over in fits of laughter. I told Ken I could land better than that with my hair on fire.

Ken loved money, especially my money. He sported his tacky white K.C. Motors cap, adorned with flashy gold leaves on the bill (low-class). I, on the other hand, wore a stylish black J.W. Motors cap with tasteful gold leaves (high-class). Ken bet I'd place my cap on the runway, he'd try to land on it, then he'd put his cap down, and I'd take a shot. I told him I'd take that bet and he'd regret it, cause I'm the best there's ever been. I'm known far and wide for my precise landing ability—well, maybe not in Alamogordo, but that's another story.

A sailplane has one wheel in the middle, with a brake to help stop. Ken went first. I placed my beautiful black cap in the center of the runway, fearless of its destruction. I saw the evil sneer on his face—then realized that's just how his face looks. He tried hard to align with my cap but fell short, missing it by 10 feet. I saved my laughter until he could hear it, then amplified it with descriptions of what his precious white cap would look like after I slammed into it.

I loved winning, and though we were wasting a perfect soaring day, humiliating my best friend was sweet. As I lined up for my landing, I saw Ken place his garish white cap in the middle of the runway. By now, a crowd had gathered to witness my obliteration of Ken's manhood. I was on the brink of setting my hair on fire when I realized I was dead on target. I pulled the brake hard, aiming to skid across his cap for maximum destruction. I'm convinced I hit it square with my locked wheel, watching it fly up behind me. I stopped quickly, jumped out laughing, and heard the crowd laughing even harder. Then I noticed something peculiar: Ken was standing there in his obnoxious white K.C. Motors cap, laughing and clutching his side. I rushed to pick up the white cap I'd destroyed. Ken had taken my pristine black cap, stuffed it in a white plastic bag, and placed it on the runway. I hate him.

Chapter 18: UFO

"Someone bought the house across the street, and I already like them," I told my wife, Vickie, as I looked out the kitchen window. She glanced out and saw the couple unloading a U-Haul. Noticing the wife in short shorts and a halter top, she punched me in the arm and shot me "That Look." She wouldn't believe me no matter what I said, but I think you know me well enough to know I'm telling the truth. I hardly glanced at that hot wife with her long tan legs, big boobs, and raven hair. The reason I knew I'd like them was the guy's Harley in the driveway. That's my story, and I'm sticking to it.

I wanted to go welcome them to the neighborhood, and Vickie insisted on coming along, but first, she had to clean up. She did her hair, put on makeup, swapped my old sweatshirt and pajama bottoms for her own short shorts and halter top. As we crossed the street, Steve, the new neighbor, was ogling Vickie. By the time we reached the curb, Steve's wife, Kat, had just finished punching him in the arm. Birds of a feather flock together, so we all became fast friends. Steve and I rode many a mile together on our Harleys, while Vickie and Kat talked constantly, mostly about us.

One day, Kat came over while I was working in the garage. "Steve crashed his bike, and he wants you to come over," she said.

"Is he okay?" I asked.

"Well, he punctured a lung, broke a rib and his wrist, and bruised his tailbone," she said.

Steve was in rough shape. "What in the hell happened?" I asked him.

"I was riding down Hawkins and had just gone under I-10 when I blacked out," he said. "A sheriff behind me said I just drove off the road and crashed. I still don't know what happened."

"Well, my friend, maybe I can shine some light on what caused your crash," I said. "Let me ask you one question. Does your ass hurt?"

"Yeah, it hurts something awful," he said. "I can't sit down."

"That's just what I thought," I said. "This is gonna be hard to believe, but I've seen this very thing before. You're the victim of an alien abduction! For some reason, the aliens spotted your sweet ass and wanted to probe it—you know how lecherous aliens are. They stopped time, zapped you up to their spacecraft, and probed your ass. Then they sent you back to your Harley, but they miscalculated, and you didn't wake up until after the crash."

Steve sat there, contemplating what I'd said. Then, for the first time since the wreck, he started laughing. Any doctor will tell you that with a broken rib, laughter's the worst thing you can do. Too late. He couldn't stop, even though the pain brought tears to his eyes. Kat thought he was having a seizure. When he finally calmed down, tears streaming down his cheeks, he started telling Kat what I'd said. When he got to the anal probing part, he lost it again. Kat grabbed me by the ear and led me to the front door.

Steve told everyone the "UFO anal probe story." He got so good at it, he told it better than me. At our next neighborhood barbecue, he had everyone in stitches, adding his own spin about the aliens' shiny probe machine.

After the Terlingua Flash's mishap lit up the pits, the Enduro's chaos never slowed. Pepper's ranch was a magnet for oddballs, and that year, a quiet man in black rolled in on a beat-up satin black Suzuki, and a scam to psyche out his competition.

Chapter 19: The Terlingua Flash and Velvet Jones

Desert racers are an eclectic bunch; *gnarly* would be a good word to describe them. Every year, we'd pile into trucks and head to the wild, dusty heart of Terlingua for the legendary Terlingua Enduro, hosted on a sprawling, sun-scorched ranch owned by a grizzled old rancher named Pepper, whose land lay just west of the majestic Big Bend National Park. Pepper had what you'd call a Western drawl. I once introduced him to a friend from New York, Saul Faultfinder, who flew in to race the Enduro. It was funny because neither could understand a word the other said. Pepper asked Saul, "Whereabouts you from, boy? You from England?" Saul shot me a quizzical look. So, I translated in my perfect speech, "Where you from, son?" leaving out the England bit. He responded, looking at me, "Yo, I'm from B'klyn, fuhgeddaboudit!" I turned to Pepper, who was waiting for a translation. "He's from Brooklyn." The conversation went on for a few minutes, each waiting for my translation, which was strange—we were all speaking English. Saul and Pepper became good friends, not brought together by a common language but by a shared love of Cazadores Tequila, of which Saul had an endless supply. All weekend, Pepper would haul his West Texas compadres over and say, "Y'all listen to my ol' buddy Saul jaw a spell. Then tell me what he's sayin'."

The Terlingua Enduro was 125 miles of cow trails and dry creek beds. This adrenaline-pumping race, set against rugged desert canyons and towering, copper-hued mesas carved over eons by creeks with their steam-shovel power, attracted a wild, roaring crowd of 600 riders. Their bikes kicked up clouds of red earth under the endless Texas sky, where a giant cumulus cloud that didn't top out at 50,000 feet was just a puff. The stars at night were so close you could point them out with I don't know how Pepper enticed them to shine so brightly, but he did take credit for it. The race was held alongside the iconic Terlingua Chili Cook-Off on the same weathered patch of Pepper's ranch, it was the grandest spectacle in the Big Bend region—a raucous, drunken celebration of speed, spice, and untamed frontier spirit, with its eclectic mix of millionaires, prostitutes, pastors, drug smugglers, Bandidos, and desert racers.

One year, I loaded my motorhome with some friends: Al Tocterman, a Midland oilman; TT LaRose, a train engineer; Rick Arron, whose occupation was a mystery; and David Berryhill, whose job was equally unclear. We were men; we didn't talk about shit like that. My lovely bride (LB), Vickie, made us a huge pan of her world-famous spaghetti, saying all I had to do was heat it up and serve it. We also had six cases of Pacifico beer, which would make us real popular at the race. I was the designated driver because I don't drink. We damn near starved that first night—Vickie forgot to mention adding water before heating. That's the night I invented the now-famous "burn-baked spaghetti." Both Berryhill and Pepper's goats seemed to like it.

An enduro is a timed event, starting with four riders every minute from 8:00 AM. Rick Arron was a peculiar fellow. He took a '54 Studebaker pickup slapped a 500-cubic-inch Cadillac motor in it, and painted it satin black. His 250 Suzuki? Also, satin black, spokes, handlebars, everything, even his gas can. He raced in black long-sleeve overalls. Two minutes before his start, he reached into his pocket, pulled out a pint of Black Velvet Whisky, chugged the whole bottle, placed his hand under his armpit, shouted, "NIT, NIT, NIT!" and tossed the bottle into a dry creek, where it shattered into a million pieces. After that show, nobody on his minute or behind him wanted to get close. We all knew the truth, and I nearly fell off my bike laughing—it wasn't whisky, just watered-down Coke. From that day forward, everyone called him "The Black Velvet."

TT LaRose was a great guy, always decked out in leathers and a shiny helmet, but in all the years we knew him, he never raced. When asked, "TT, you racing pro or amateur today?" he'd reply, "I only dress this way to pick up girls." Come to think of it, that wasn't a bad idea. Racing motorcycles was the best way I knew to meet nurses, but there were plenty of unattached girls in the pits when the men were racing, and no stitches required.

David Berryhill, a friend from the oil fields just north of Imperial, Texas, was as goofy as a football bat. His girlfriend, who everyone called "Fud," was a walking tattoo gallery, later the poster child for every Austin waitress. The first time I met David, he had a colonel's Army Delta Force uniform hanging behind the seat of his '56 International pickup. He claimed a mental breakdown in the Grenada War got him a medical discharge. I assumed he was telling the truth—his craziness was obvious. He liked to race in what he called "commando gear," full desert camo and desert boots. Until that day, I didn't realize his definition of "going commando" meant no underwear.

Normally, that wouldn't come up, but in a 125-mile enduro, you refuel twice. David was a dandy, living in a 1950s single-wide mobile home with better tires on the roof than on his pickup. He had no washer or dryer, and the Pecos River, 10 feet from his front door, tasted like the Russian Army had sneezed in it. His leathers *stank*. At mile 70, David hit a pucker bush and pulled a "Flying W", both feet off the pegs, straight up in the air, spread wide. The move was too much for his rotten leathers, which split from knee to knee. Remember, he was commando. Quitting an enduro is for sissies, but he needed gas.

The pit was in a valley by a stream, set there so wives and kids could play in the crystal-clear water while waiting. David faced a conundrum: quit or refuel, he'd expose himself. He squeezed his legs together, thankful for once that he wasn't well-endowed, a fact soon to be public. His five-gallon gas can sat alone. He pulled up cautiously, knowing that getting off to refuel would reveal his "Johnson" to everyone. He tried to get attention, but everyone was busy, so he whistled, loud and shrill, like a steam engine. That got more eyes than he wanted. Two guys and three women came over. "Ladies, I had an accident, and I don't want to cause a scene, so would you avert your eyes while one of you gentlemen pours gas into my tank?" It didn't go smoothly. The men called more people over, and the women pointed and laughed. David gripped the situation with both hands. He'd killed the bike without thinking how he'd stand to kick-start it with a hundred eyes on him.

When a guy took off David's gas cap and lifted the can to pour, the nozzle came off, dumping five gallons of gas on David's exposed crotch. The pain must've been excruciating, I've never had gas dumped on my crotch, so I wouldn't know, but Berryhill claims it's torture. Forgetting decency, he screamed like his balls were on fire, fell off the bike, scrambled to his feet, and ran to the creek, hollering the whole way. As he sat in the cooling water, Pepper walked up and asked if he wanted a light. Everyone laughed at his pain, but Pepper loaded David's bike into his truck and took him back to camp. That day lives in infamy, and David became known as the "Terlingua Flash."

Next, you'll learn a valuable lesson on how to beat a speeding ticket.

Chapter 20: Flying Snake and Blimp Defense

Growing up on the wide-open plains of West Texas, I honed my silver tongue to wriggle out of trouble faster than a jackrabbit dodging a coyote. Texans don't just tolerate a good story; they crave it, like a bowl of Chico's Tacos in El Paso. A lie's just a lie unless you wrap it in a yarn so colorful it could make a rattlesnake blush. That's when it becomes a *tale*, the kind that might just soften the heart of a stone-faced highway patrolman once did an informal study of the fib's folks spin to dodge a speeding ticket, based on driver polls, police logs, and late-night chats at the diner. The classics never die: "I didn't know the speed limit" (sure, buddy, those signs are just roadside art); "I'm late for work" (because your boss loves that excuse); "Rushing to the hospital" (hope it's not for a broken fibula from all that stretching); "Everyone else was speeding" (classic herd mentality); "The ice cream's melting in the car" (a personal favorite—who can argue with dessert distress?); and, of course, "I gotta pee real bad" (officers must hear that one five times a shift). Surveys from CarInsurance.com and AAA say only about 12% of drivers outright lie, but those who do stick to these hits. Success? Maybe 50% for the believable ones, but if the cop smells bull, you're toast. Polite honesty and a plea for a warning work better than a tall tale gone wrong. So, if you can't fake sincerity don't even try this.

Growing up on the wide-open plains of West Texas, I honed my silver tongue to wriggle out of trouble faster than a jackrabbit dodging a coyote. Texans don't just tolerate a good story; they crave it. A lie's just a lie unless you wrap it in a yarn so colorful it could make a rattlesnake blush. That's when it becomes a *tale*, the kind that might just soften the heart of a stone-faced highway patrolman once did an informal study of the fib's folks spin to dodge a speeding ticket, based on driver polls, police logs, and late-night chats at the diner. The classics never die: "I didn't know the speed limit" (sure, buddy, those signs are just roadside art); "I'm late for work" (because your boss loves that excuse); "Rushing to the hospital" (hope it's not for a broken fibula from all that stretching); "Everyone else was speeding" (classic herd mentality); "The ice cream's melting in the car" (a personal favorite—who can argue with dessert distress?); and, of course, "I gotta pee real bad" (officers must hear that one five times a shift). Surveys from CarInsurance.com and AAA say only about 12% of drivers outright lie, but those who do stick to these hits. Success? Maybe 50% for the believable ones, but if the cop smells bull, you're toast. Polite honesty and a plea for a warning work better than a tall tale gone wrong.

Let me take you back to where this all began, at Sara's Café, where the enchiladas are spicy and the gossip is spicier. I was scarfing down my lunch when I overheard County Judge Freddy Capers at the next table, chowing on chili rellenos and griping to his buddy. Freddy, a short-statured cowboy with a Stetson as big as his reputation, he had a startling resemblance to a thumb tack was fed up. "Every dang speeder tells me the same tired excuses," he grumbled, stabbing a relleno. "If someone spins me a story I ain't heard before, I swear I'll dismiss their ticket on the spot."

My ears perked up like a dog hearing a can opener. A Get Out of Jail Free card? In West Texas? That was the Magna Carta, Declaration of Independence, and a cold Pacifico rolled into one. West Texas, for those who've never had the pleasure, is flatter than a pancake and twice as wide. They say if your dog runs off, you can watch him hightail it for a week. Distance ain't measured in miles out here—it's hours or six-packs. Odessa? An hour away. Midland? A six-pack. Back then, the speed limit was a soul-crushing 55 MPH, which felt like a personal insult to common sense. Driving 55 to Odessa took an hour and a half, but at my preferred 85, it was a breezy 45 minutes. Sure, my lead foot meant I was a regular donor to the county treasury—call it a "common sense tax," not a ticket. But Freddy's proclamation lit a fire under me. I could use my God-given gift for Texas-sized tales to zip around at 85 without emptying my wallet. To quote MLK (with apologies), "Free at last! "My first shot came not in Pecos County but in Jeff Davis County, cruising back from El Paso on I-10. A trooper clocked me at 85 in a 55 near Fort

Hancock. Figuring judges everywhere must be as bored as Freddy, I penned a letter to the court, pouring on the charm like syrup on a stack of pancakes:

Dear Honorable Judge,

My name is J.E. Warr, and I was ticketed in your county for doing 85 in a 55. In the spirit of honesty, I was indeed hauling tail. But in these tough times, I humbly ask to take Defensive Driving instead of paying a fine. If you insist on justice, I'll have no choice but to sell my kids' pet pony to the dog food factory to pay the fine.

Sincerely,

J.E. Warr

A week later, a notice arrived: "Take Defensive Driving." Hot dang, it worked! I sauntered over to my buddy, the city judge, sweet-talked her into a Defensive Driving certificate, and sent it off. I was unstoppable, like a tumbleweed in a windstorm. Emboldened, I soon found myself in hot water again, this time barreling down Highway 1053 at 85 MPH. Cresting a rise, I spotted a DPS trooper's cruiser. I slammed the brakes, but it was too late. He swaggered up, tipped his hat, and drawled, "Son, that's the fastest I've seen a truck go without its wheels turnin'." Ticket in hand, I knew it was showtime. Next day, I strolled into Freddy's courtroom. He was hunched over paperwork, but when he saw me, a grin spread across his face like butter on hot cornbread. "Hey, Warr, what's up?" he called. I launched into my tale. "Freddy, I was the victim of a cruel practical joke. I was cruisin' down 1053, windows down, singin' along to a Merle Haggard song on KPFS AM radio like I like to do, when a damn Mesa Flying Snake, you know, those sneaky devils, flew right into my cab!" Freddy's eyebrow shot up. "I'm deathly afraid of snakes, so I stomped its head, but wouldn't you know it, its noggin got wedged between my foot and the gas pedal." I paused for effect. "Then what happened?" Freddy asked. I slid the ticket onto his bench. If I would have lifted my foot off that snake, I wouldn't be here today. Freddy leaned back, puzzled, then chuckled. "Case dismissed," he said, shaking his head. I tipped my hat, and he thanked me for the entertainment.

That only fanned the flames. A month later, I was back on 1053, this time pushing 90. Same rise, same DPS cruiser. Busted again. I marched into Freddy's court, ready to dazzle. He spotted me and waved me over. "You got another tale, Warr?" Before I could start, he grabbed the PA mic. "Attention, folks! Warr's about to spin a yarn. Get

to my courtroom if you want to hear it firsthand!" Twenty secretaries, sheriff's deputies, and assorted locals' people in, grinning like kids at a county fair. I cleared my throat. "Freddy, I was rollin' down 1053, windows down…""Were you singing along like you like to do?" "Yes just like I like to.", when a shadow darkened the sky. I slowed down, looked up, and—Lord help me—it was the Goodyear Blimp, low as a buzzard! The pilot hollered, 'Clear the road ahead, we're out of gas and need to land!" The crowd snickered. "Now, Freddy, you know how safety conscience? So I floored it to clear the way. But as I crested that rise, a DPS trooper nabbed me." I slapped the ticket on his bench, then added, "And that dang blimp pilot? He yelled 'SUCKER!' as he flew off!" The courtroom erupted in laughter. Freddy banged his gavel. "Case dismissed!" he roared, wiping tears from his eyes.

I was on a roll, practically a West Texas legend. So, when the Jaycees announced a liars' contest, I strutted in, certain I'd take the crown. I retold my Mesa Flying Snake and Goodyear Blimp tales to a crowd of hundreds, milking every laugh. But then Freddy stood up, all five-foot-nothing of him, and bellowed, "He ain't lying', he's tellin' the truth!" The crowd howled, but my dreams of victory crashed like a cheap pickup. In West Texas, a good tale's worth more than a trophy—it's currency, freedom, and a story to tell over enchiladas for years to come.

No Texas tales can be complete without at least one ghost story.

Chapter 21: Vampires, Witches and Ghost

My good friend Clyde, better known as "Catchit" to everyone in Archer City, Texas, earned his nickname on the football field. Playing for the Archer City High School Wildcats, if a football was thrown his way and he could touch it, he'd catch it. We were cruising to Dallas to watch the Cowboys beat the hell out of the Redskins on Halloween day when I brought up ghosts. Catchit grinned and launched into this tale.

"I was fresh off the farm in Archer City, Texas, but landed a football scholarship at the University of Texas. I read a book once—didn't like it. I ain't stupid, just not book smart. Never cared a lick for Shakespeare, science, or algebra. Catching footballs, now that's my game. They tested me and found I'm dyslexic—so bad I tell folks I'm 'lexcdystic.' They say nature compensates, and dyslexics are often have good at math or pattern recognition skills. Math ain't my thing, but I'm damn good at reading patterns in a pass defense. That's what got me a full ride at Texas, and why I pick easy classes like MUS 307 (*Jazz Appreciation*). Light assignments, fun material, and exams you can ace if you show up. Professor Bryant's version is a breeze, or so I heard. Then there's EDP 350L (*Human Sexuality*), all online with writing prompts and quizzes—no exams in some sections. I also took INF 322T (*Children's Literature*), reading graphic novels and *Gulliver's Travels* with weekly quizzes and a comic for the final project. It's fun, low-stress, perfect for a guy like me. My favorite, though, is CC 304D (*Classical Mythology/Occult*), diving into myths, ghosts, and spooky stuff from ancient times. These classes are tough to get into but easy to pass—especially when you're a Heisman Trophy candidate, and strings get pulled.

Growing up, everybody I knew believed in chupacabras and ghosts. We'd hunt whenever we could, sitting around a campfire, dipping snuff, and swapping ghost stories. Everyone swore their tale was true, and hell, I even believed some of mine. My daddy always said a fool's someone who lies to themselves and believes it. Those campfire nights made me think a class on ghosts would be a blast.

On the first day of CC 304D, I took a seat in the back of the auditorium, so no one would see me spit my snuff on the floor. No spit can for me—farm habits die hard, even if the girls wrinkle their noses. Over a hundred kids packed the room, all chasing that easy 'A.' Professor Learnod, a short guy in a brown tweed suit with unnaturally large hands, took the stage, his eyes glinting like he knew something we didn't. 'Who among you has had an experience with witches, evil spirits, or ghosts?' he asked, voice low and sharp. Some frat guys in front joked about ex-girlfriends being witches, fishing for laughs. Nobody took them seriously.

Professor Smith got serious and told us this story. 'In the shadowed heart of the Louisiana bayou, where gnarled cypress trees claw at the moon and the air hums with restless spirits, the name Marie Laveau is whispered only in dread. No soul dares speak it aloud, for fear her shadow might stir; they say if you ever let her shadow touch you are doomed . She's no mere woman, she's the Witch Queen, a voodoo sorceress whose eyes burn like embers through the swamp's choking mist. Her voice, a hiss slithering through the reeds, can bind your soul or unravel it entirely. She at one time had her heart smashed by a man and she blames them all for it.

'Deep in the mire, where the water's black as sin, Marie's shack looms, a rotting throne of bones and charms. The air reeks of sulfur and decay, the ground pulsing with the screams of those who crossed her. She weaves spells with a flick of her wrist, her fingers trailing shadows that choke the life from men. Handsome Jack, a fool with a silver tongue, thought he could outwit her. He came with lies, promising love, but his laughter turned to screams as the swamp swallowed him whole. *Another man done gone,* she cackled, her voice splitting the night like a blade.

'Her power ain't no parlor trick. Snakes coil at her feet, their eyes glowing like hellfire. Owls screech her name, and the wind carries her curses to those who defy her. One wrong step, one whispered doubt, and she'll weave your name into her gris-gris bag. You'll feel it, your breath stolen, your shadow torn away, your body sinking into the mire as the bayou claims you. *Another man done gone,* she'll sing, her laugh a jagged edge haunting your dreams. And beware, stranger, if you tread those cursed paths. If Marie Laveau's eyes lock onto yours, cold as a grave, and she offers her hand in marriage, don't dare run. Stay, or you'll vanish into the swamp's hungry maw, your screams just another note in her endless, unholy song. This ain't no campfire ghost story, no friendly Casper. This is the stuff of legends, raw, bone-chilling truths that'll drag you from your warm bed at midnight, heart pounding, to check your locked doors. Because out there, in the dark, Marie Laveau is waiting.'

Then he flipped a switch, dimming the stage lights, and lit a dusty candle that flickered like it was alive. His voice dropped, slow and eerie, his smile—damn, it was evil, like something dark hid behind it. He glided across the stage, eyes scanning the crowd like a hawk picking prey. 'Let me tell you about a vampire,' he said, his words curling through the air like smoke.

'In New Orleans' French Quarter, where gas lamps flicker and jazz hums through the humid night, Elias roamed. A vampire since the Civil War, he wasn't your typical monster. His amber eyes held sorrow, not menace. He fed only on the dying, their blood a bitter need. He called it "civilized," like he was doing them a favor. One night, in a crumbling Creole townhouse, he found

Margot, a beautiful painter dying of consumption, abandoned by her so-called friends. Her pulse fluttered like a trapped moth, her skin pale as the stained smock she clutched. She didn't scream when she saw him. "You're the one from my dreams," she whispered. Elias froze, feeling hunted for the first time. Her paintings, scattered on the floor, showed his face—his sharp jaw, his haunted gaze—sketched in fevered strokes. She'd never met him, but she knew him, and she waited with something rare: hope.

"'Why me?" he asked, kneeling beside her. Margot coughed, blood on her lips, stirring his hunger. An evil smile crept across his face. "You're my last guest," she said, her bloody teeth gleaming. She offered her wrist, fearless, like she'd been waiting for his kiss. Elias hadn't turned anyone in a century—the curse of eternal life was too heavy. But her defiant spark woke something in him, a long-dead hope. Hope had brought them together. He drank, her blood warm and sweet, full of life and promise. Then he bit his wrist, letting one drop of eternity fall to her lips. She gasped, her body shuddering as the change took hold. By dawn, Margot stood, no longer frail, her eyes glowing like his, that same evil smile curling her lips. "Paint the world with me in the moonlight," she said. Elias felt the weight of forever lighten. They vanished into the bayou, two shadows bound by blood and art, leaving only her final canvas: Elias, smiling, no longer alone.'

I was hooked, leaning forward, snuff forgotten. This class was gonna be fun—hell, I wanted to invite the professor to go hunting with us. Leanard's candle flickered as he grinned, pointing at the crowd. 'How many of you believe in vampires?' Ten hands went up. He zeroed in on a guy named Jimmy, handing him the candle. Apparently, you had to hold it to speak. 'Tell us your vampire story.'

Jimmy, a skinny kid with nervous eyes, cleared his throat. 'One night, I was walking my girlfriend, Lena, home from a diner. It was past midnight; the October air was so cold our breath fogged. We cut through Oakwood Cemetery a short cut you should never take. At iron gates something that looked like skeletal fingers in the moonlight. Lena laughed nervously about ghosts, but I felt uneasy, like something was watching. As we passed the headstones, a prickle hit my spine. The shadows moved—not with the wind or moon, but like they had a mind, pooling, like a gaggle of crows at the edge of my sight.

'"Did you hear that?" Lena whispered, slowing down. A rustle, like dry leaves, echoed behind us. I turned, nothing, but the shadows by the fence writhed, stretching like smoky tendrils. "Let's go," I said, pulling her. The air got heavy, the rustle turning into a low, guttural hum coming from everywhere. Lena's eyes went wide. "Jimmy, it's following us." I saw it, a shape forming from the shadows, tall and lean, its edges blurring into the night. Its eyes glowed like embers in a face too pale to be human. My heart pounded as I grabbed her hand and ran. It didn't chase like a person; it glided, flickering between graves, closing in without effort.

"'It's a vampire," Lena gasped, her voice shaking as we sprinted. I didn't argue, it felt ancient, hungry, like a nightmare come alive. The shadows pulsed, the hum now a snarl that shook my bones. Ahead, St. David's Episcopal Church's steeple cut the sky, its doors glowing under a cross-shaped lantern. "Get to the church!" I yelled. We stumbled up the steps, the air freezing as the thing sharpened into a gaunt figure with claws like black knives. It wasn't evil, just hungry. Lena fumbled with the door, hands trembling. By some miracle, it opened as the vampire lunged, its snarl cut off as we slammed it shut. The church's silence swallowed us, only our gasps and a faint hymn echoing with a power that even this creature respected.

'Outside, shadows pressed against the stained-glass windows, swirling like ink, but it didn't cross the threshold. Lena clung to me, whispering, "We're safe." The altar's cross gleamed, and the vampire's hum faded. We stayed till dawn, sleeping in the pews. When we left, the shadows were gone, but I swear I saw ember eyes watching from the cemetery, waiting for another night. You'll think I'm lying, but I double dog dare you to walk by that graveyard at midnight and prove me wrong.'

The class was silent, spooked. Leanard's grin widened, like he fed off our fear. 'Next,' he said, 'who believes in ghosts?' Twenty hands shot up, including mine. 'Have any of you had sex with a ghost?' I raised my hand, caught up in the moment. He pointed at me and called me down to the stage. 'You, in the back—come forward and tell us about the time you had sex with a ghost.'

I shuffled to the stage, my face burning as two hundred eyes drilled into me. My sneakers squeaked on the polished floor, each step heavier than the last. My heart pounded, a clammy sweat prickling my skin. I gripped the candle, wax dripping hot onto my trembling fingers, stinging like my growing regret. I'd gotten myself into this mess, and it was up to me to get out. 'Man, this is mortifying,' I stammered, scratching my neck raw. 'I totally misunderstood what you said.' My voice cracked, a nervous laugh escaping, echoing in the dead-quiet room. My cheeks flamed hotter, and I wished I could melt into the stage floor, the weight of my blunder heavier than any ghost story

I didn't have. After a moment of eerie silence, for some stupid reason, I told the truth: 'I don't have a story about making love to a ghost; I thought you said sex with a *goat*.' I spoke louder than necessary. I'd never seen so many open mouths in my life. The room erupted in laughter. I'm not gonna tell you my nickname after that, but it rhymes with 'Goat Trucker.' I did get that A."